THOUGHT CATALOG BOOKS

Shadowhunters & Myths

Shadowhunters & Myths

Discovering the Legends Behind The Mortal Instruments

VALERIE ESTELLE FRANKEL

Thought Catalog Books

Brooklyn, NY

THOUGHT CATALOG BOOKS

Copyright © 2016 by Valerie Estelle Frankel

All rights reserved. Published by Thought Catalog Books, a division of The Thought & Expression Co., Williamsburg, Brooklyn. Founded in 2010, Thought Catalog is a website and imprint dedicated to your ideas and stories. We publish fiction and non-fiction from emerging and established writers across all genres. For general information and submissions: manuscripts@thoughtcatalog.com.

First edition, 2016

ISBN 978-0692672938

10 9 8 7 6 5 4 3 2 1

Cover design by © KJ Parish

Contents

Introduction		1
1.	What Are Angels?	3
2.	Runes and Adamic Language	11
3.	Lexicon of the More Famous Angels	19
4.	The Nature of Demons	35
5.	Protections	45
6.	Holy Symbols	53
7.	Demon Hierarchy	65
8.	Greater Demons	69
9.	Demonarium	91
10.	Other Creatures	113
11.	Downworlders	117
12.	Witches and Warlocks	121
13.	Vampires	123
14.	Werewolves	129
15.	Fairies	139
16.	Bible, Myth, and Other Lore	155
17.	The Film	191
18.	The Show	193
19.	The Next Series	197
Works Cited		203
About the Author		209

Introduction

The bestselling *Mortal Instruments* series got a huge boost with its film *City of Bones* and again with the television show *Shadowhunters*. What's the secret to its popularity?

Like *Harry Potter,* it heavily incorporates world myth, adding a context through which it all could be true. Of course, Shadowhunters don't cast spells – only use runes of angelic power and call on angels to bless their seraph blades. As such, this series comes closer than *Harry Potter* to Christian theology, and even more – Jewish. The angels and demons come straight from medieval angelologies and demonologies, with lots of Bible quotes and Jewish mysticism as well. There's not only demonic Lilith and Samael's attack of demon hordes, but the Marks themselves –much like angelic blessings, secret languages, and protective symbols of the Old World. Likewise, Clare's Angel Raziel with his runes and Mortal Instruments is based on the mythic Raziel, keeper of secrets, and his famous book. With heavenly fire, the Mark of Cain, and the original language of heaven, there are countless more references, all fully explained in this volume. Adding in demons straight from Johann Weyer's *Pseudomonarchia Daemonum,* the series has strong roots in history and legend.

Clare also brings in the hell of Dante and fallen angels of Milton with long lists of poetry in her chapter titles and the Victorian prequels called *The Infernal Devices* series. Her fairies are straight from the world of Holly Black's *Tithe,* but also that of famous poetry on the Wild Hunt, Thomas the

1

Rhymer, and Tam Lin. Mixed in are European mermaids and nixies, and in a wider scope, djinn from the Middle East, satyrs from Greece, Japanese oni, Caribbean zombies, and far more species, all straight from the ancient legends.

All stories are true, Shadowhunters say. And this book offers the folktales and archaic lore revealing the ancient knowledge behind them.

This guide provides background on the Shadowhunters' world. Thus it does spoil the books, while providing extra lore behind them. At the time of writing, there are two main series: The Mortal Instruments stars Clary, Jace, Alec, Isabelle, Magnus, and their friends in modern New York – six books, one film, and one ongoing television show (renamed Shadowhunters). The other, a prequel series from a century earlier, features parabatai Will Herondale and James Carstairs, along with the mysteriously gifted Tessa Grey, all in the London Institute. The characters are interlinked by themes and artifacts as well as genealogy, and reading them all is highly recommended. Within this world are Magnus Bane and Simon Lewis short story collections, several guide books edited and written by author Cassandra Clare and her friends, and many of Clare's blog posts and online excerpts. The next series, The Dark Artifices, arrives soon, focusing on the Los Angeles Institute a few years after Clary and Jace's final sixth book triumph. It's a complex world, brimming with content and devotion to detail, more of which is explored within these pages.

1

What Are Angels?

Of all the celestial beings, seraphim, cherubim, and archangels, angels are closest to earth and earthly matters, and intercede between God and Man. They watch over households and individuals, guiding them subtlety and protecting them from demons. They are also messengers and carry God's word to mankind. In Hebrew, they are called *mal'akh*, "messenger," in Persian, *angaros* or "courier." "Angelus" is Latin for messenger. A 6000 year old stele (in archeology, an inscribed upright stone slab or column) from Ur bears the oldest recorded image of an angel. It's pouring the water of life into a goblet held by a king (Webster x). Tomas Aquinas notes that the lowest order of angels guards individuals, whereas, according to Gregory's opinion:

> (…)the more universal an agent is, the higher it is.
> Thus the guardianship of the human race belongs
> to the order of "Principalities," or perhaps to the
> "Archangels," whom we call the angel princes (…)
> Moreover all corporeal creatures are guarded by
> the "Virtues"; and likewise the demons by the
> "Powers," and the good spirits by the "Principali-
> ties."
> (Aquinas 113.3)

In the Bible, angels do not have free will but only bring messages or fulfill a single task. Angels also do not enter filthy places nor places where a person is not dressed decently, because angels are good and shy by nature. Some angels are dedicated to a particular person to record their deeds.

Ithuriel tells Tessa, "I am an angel of the divine...brother to the Sijil, Kurabi, and the Zurah, the Fravashis and Dakinis (*Clockwork Princess* 396). Sijil, Kurabi, and the Zurah are names for Islamic angels, while the Fravashis are protective spirits from the ancient Persian religion, and the Dakinis, angelic Buddhist beings. Angels or their equivalent indeed appear worldwide as intercessors between man and God.

Clockwork Prince's Chapter Ten is called "The Virtue of Angels" from a famous quote from the Bible commentary the Talmud: "The virtue of angels is that they cannot deteriorate; their flaw is that they cannot improve. Man's flaw is that he can deteriorate; and his virtue is that he can improve" ("Clockwork Prince Cover and Chapter Titles"). Thus angels here are circumscribed by their inability. In this tradition, a released *Dark Artifices* snippet subverts angelic goodness:

> *"Let me tell you a truth before you die, Emma,"*
> *said the voice. "It is a secret about the Nephilim.*
> *They hate love, human love, because they were*
> *born of angels. And while God charged his angels*
> *to take care of humans, the angels were made first,*
> *and they have always hated God's second creation.*
> *That is why Lucifer fell. He was an angel who*
> *would not bow to mankind, God's favored child.*
> *Love is the weakness of human beings, and the*

*Angels despise them for it, and the Clave despises
it too, and therefore they punish it. Do you know
what happens to parabatai who fall in love? Do
you know why it's forbidden?"*

Angels cannot change man's free will, but they can inspire or
persuade him, in dreams or in person. When Moses asked:
"Show me Thy glory," the angel answered: "I will show thee all
good" (Exodus 33:18-19).

> *Therefore an angel does not move the will suffi-
> ciently, either as the object or as showing the
> object. But he inclines the will as something lov-
> able, and as manifesting some created good
> ordered to God's goodness. And thus he can incline
> the will to the love of the creature or of God, by
> way of persuasion.*
> (Aquinas 106.2)

The Bible calls angels "ministering spirits" in Hebrews 1:14,
and believers say that God has made each angel in the way
that would best empower that angel to serve the people whom
God loves. The Bible says in 2 Samuel 14:20 that God has
given angels the knowledge about "all things that are on the
earth." God has also created angels with the power to see
the future. In Daniel 10:14, an angel tells the prophet Daniel:
"Now I have come to explain to you what will happen to your
people in the future, for the vision concerns a time yet to
come."

At the same time, angels are God's champions, the generals of his army. Magnus tells Simon that angels are more than messengers – they're soldiers. The angels who overturned Sodom, "struck the people of Sodom with blindness or aorasia [dazzlement], so that they could not find the door" (Genesis 19:11).

The three books of Enoch are one of the top sources for Judeo-Christian angels and fallen angels. Another is the fifth century *The Celestial Hierarchy* by Dionysus the Aeorpagite. St. Thomas Aquinas used his hierarchy of angels in his own thirteenth century work, *Summa Theologiae*. Medieval grimoires such as *The Lesser Key of Solomon* contain much on angels and demons as well. *The Celestial Hierarchy* sorts angels thus:

First Choir

1. Seraphim
2. Cherubim
3. Thrones

   Second Choir

4. Dominations
5. Virtues
6. Powers

   Third Choir

7. Principalities
8. Archangels
9. Angels

Paradise Lost adds: "Hear all ye Angels, Progenie of Light/ Thrones, Dominations, Princedoms, Vertues, Powers/ Hear my Decree, which unrevok't shall stand" (V:600-602). Aquinas explains:

The name "Seraphim" is derived from ardor,
which pertains to charity; and the name "Cheru-
bim" from knowledge… the name "Seraphim" is
found in Isaiah 6:2; the name "Cherubim" in
Ezekiel 1 (Cf. 10:15-20); "Thrones" in Colossians
1:16; "Dominations," "Virtues," "Powers," and
"Principalities" are mentioned in Ephesians 1:21;
the name "Archangels" in the canonical epistle of
St. Jude (9), and the name "Angels" is found in
many places of Scripture.
(Aquinas 106.5)

Angels, the lowest rank, are the closest to humanity and thus
beings we can relate best to. Their chiefs, like Michael and
Gabriel, are archangels. The Archangels act as God's messengers at the most critical times and stand before the Throne of
God (Luke 1:26). Here is the list from the *Book of Enoch*, one
of the earliest. In it, there are seven archangels (*irin we-kad-*
dishin, "holy ones who watch"):

And these are the names of the holy angels who
watch. Uriel, one of the holy angels, who is over
the world and over Tartarus. Raphael, one of the
holy angels, who is over the spirits of men. Raguel,
one of the holy angels who takes vengeance on the
world of the luminaries. Michael, one of the holy
angels, to wit, he that is set over the best part of
mankind [and] over chaos. Saraqâêl, one of the
holy angels, who is set over the spirits, who sin in
the spirit. Gabriel, one of the holy angels, who is

over Paradise and the serpents and the Cherubim.
Remiel, one of the holy angels, whom God set over
those who rise.
(20:1-8)

Judaism, Christianity, and Islam all believe in the concept of guardian angels: one angel who watches over each person all their lives. Quotes from their various holy books support this belief:

> *He hath given His angels charge over thee, to keep*
> *thee in all thy ways.*
> (Psalm 90:11)

> *Jesus said: Take heed that ye despise not one of*
> *these little ones; for I say unto you, That in heaven*
> *their angels do always behold the face of my*
> *Father which is in heaven.*
> (Matthew 18:10)

> *There is no human being but has a protector over*
> *him* (or her) (i.e. angels in charge of each human
> being guarding him, writing his good and bad
> deeds, etc.).
> (Qur'an 86:4)

One can try to guess the name of his or her angel: some correspond to particular days and zodiac signs, while others are the patrons of certain professions or callings. Shadowhunters are versatile, calling on strength, cleverness, protection, healing, and a variety of other abilities. Thus, most Shadowhunters name their blades for a variety of angels, invoking the protection of the entire divine host. Of course, Tessa has a specific guardian angel inside her necklace – Ithuriel. Jace and Alec call on Ithuriel, as well as Michael and Raphael at specific times to invoke very specific and extremely powerful divine protection.

According to Shadowhunter lore, in 1000 AD, the mortals Jonathan, Abigail, and David were battling a demon invasion. Overwhelmed and drowning in a lake, Jonathan prayed for help. Raziel rose from Lake Lyn, holding the Mortal Instruments. Jonathan asked him to save his comrades, and Raziel slew all the demons, and then presented the tools to Jonathan so he might create the race of Shadowhunters to protect earth's innocents.

Certainly, the angel Raziel created the Shadowhunters and has a tie to them. However, even the Shadowhunters have difficulty summoning angels. Using the Mortal Instruments as a set they would try, but very rarely. Angels cannot maintain their corporeal form on Earth for long, and more to the point, are often wrathful at being forced to manifest. There are ways to bind an angel as one would a demon, but these are considered horrifically blasphemous. Valentine uses these to imprison Ithuriel and compel Raziel. Magnus explains in *Lost Souls:*

> *"There's a reason the ritual of the Mortal Instruments was so complicated." Magnus made the sugar bowl float over to himself and dumped some of the white powder into his coffee. "Angels act at*

the behest of God, not human beings—not even Shadowhunters. Summon one, and you're likely to find yourself blasted with divine wrath. The whole point of the Mortal Instruments ritual wasn't that it allowed someone to summon Raziel. It was that it protected the summoner from the Angel's wrath once he did appear."

While there are other ways besides the Mortal Instruments to summon an angel, they protect the summoner from divine wrath. The Mark of Cain of course can do likewise.

2

Runes and Adamic Language

For Shadowhunters, runes are a complex language given to them by the Angel Raziel and recorded in the Book of the Covenant, and copied in the Grey Book. Jace adds, "Gray is short for 'Gramarye.' It means 'magic, hidden wisdom.' In it is copied every rune the Angel Raziel wrote in the original Book of the Covenant. There aren't many copies because each one has to be specially made. Some of the runes are so powerful they'd burn through regular pages" (*City of Bones*). This alphabet, inscribed on the skin, grants them powers beyond those of mundanes. Strength, speed, stealth, protection, healing – all these are granted to them so they can battle demons and protect mankind. Clare adds:

> *Runes are not "things you draw on yourself that give you power." Runes are letters, or ideograms, or anyway part of a larger language system. We don't know or understand the angelic language that the Gray Book runes are in, because we are incapable of doing so as humans. (It's implied that Clary's rune-making power may come from having some unconscious intuitive grasp for the*

angelic language of the Gray Book runes.) We in
fact only know they ARE runes and not just squig-
gles because Raziel said they were runes.
(Clare Tumblr, Feb 2015)

Runes are listed in the *Shadowhunter's Codex* (Clare's guide to the Shadowhunters' world) and in several websites including these:

http://shadowhunters.wikia.com/wiki/Runes

http://www.cassandraclare.com/my-writing/excerpts-extras/runes

Clare's runes appear Arabic – a curly combination of pictographs and Hebrew.

For a long time, Biblical Hebrew was considered the original tongue, or language of Adam. The Old Testament was written in it, and therefore all of the words and prophecies that came to mankind through the ancient prophets and forefathers were in Hebrew. Thus many believed this was the same language used by God and Angels in the formation and direction of the universe.

During the Renaissance, a line of famous occultists and cryptographers began to experiment with rediscovering Adam's language in pursuit of spiritual and magical power. In the early 1500s, Heinrich Cornelius Agrippa wrote his *Three Books of Occult Philosophy*, in which he recorded three of the earliest Medieval/Renaissance examples of divine writing: Celestial, Malachim (Angelic), and Passing the River with alphabets given for encoding Divine Names upon talismans.

They all shared a great deal with Hebrew, like Clare's own rune system.

An obscure alchemical text called the *Voarchadumia*, from the mid-1500s, created a an Alphabet of Enoch, closer to Latin letters. The Angelical alphabet later recorded by Dr. John Dee and his scryer Edward Kelley is similar. Dee wrote an entire book in this script, treating it at last as a language, not just an alphabet. He believed this to be the Book of Life, the Celestial Tablets that had once been viewed by Enoch. He called it the *Book of the Speech from God* (*Loagaeth*). His Angelical Language—often called "Enochian"—has become foundational to much of Western occultism such as the Order of the Golden Dawn. The Shadowhunter runes resemble something between this and the Arabic/Hebrew letters.

Meanwhile, the word "rune" derives from the Indo-European root *ru*, "mystery or secret." The runes most commonly seen today come from the Norse tradition, with alphabetic meanings as well as symbolic ones. The Norse god Odin was said to have traded his eye for the runic language, one adapted into Tolkien and other fantasy works. Today, some people use these letters for spell casting and meditation. As the *Internet Book of Shadows* describes modern runes:

> *In the most mundane sense, runes are an alphabet much as our own alphabet and others such as the Greek and Cyrillic alphabets. Each rune represents a sound and was/is used to write words with.*

> *But that is in the most MUNDANE of senses.*

Runes were used long before the concept of writing was around. Each rune is an archetype of a force. People had concepts for such things as Fire, Honour, Birth, et.al. and each of these concepts were given names to make them easier for us to comprehend.

(...)

Runes can be used for fortune telling. They can be drawn and placed and read much like tarot cards. The can be cast or strewn and the relationship of groupings, distance and angles and patterns formed will tell the caster what he wishes to know.

Runes are also entities in and of themselves. Much like the angels, princes, demons, sylphs, undines and watchtowers of the ceremonial magician, each rune can be invoked or evoked and the power harnessed to work one's will to enlighten the intellect. They are a fantastic meditation tool and will always increase one's knowledge.

The Shadowhunters, meanwhile, specifically use the Marks given by the Angel Raziel to defend themselves, rather than actually casting spells. Their voyance runes echo protective symbols of an eye that ward off evil around the world. This similar "Kemi," or written amulet, was used by Jews in the Middle East:

Prosper me in the writing of this parchment, that it be a preservative, deliverance, protection and a perfect cure to the wearer of this Charm from sundry and divers evil diseases existing in the world, from an evil eye and an evil tongue. I adjure you all ye kinds of evil eyes, a black eye, a hazel eye, blue eye, yellow eye, short eye, broad eye, straight eye, narrow eye, deep eye, protruding eye, eye of a male, eye of a female, the eye of a wife and the eye of a husband, eye of a woman and her daughter, eye of a woman and her kinsfolk, eye of an unmarried man, eye of an old man, eye of an old woman, eye of a virgin, eye of one not a virgin, eye of a widow, eye of a married wife, eye of a divorced wife, all kinds of evil eyes in the world which looked and spoke with an evil eye concerning or against the wearer of this charm, I command and adjure you by the Most Holy and Mighty and Exalted Eye, the Only Eye, the White Eye, the Right Eye, the Compassionate the Ever Watchful and Open Eye, the Eye that never slumbereth nor sleepeth, the Eye to Which all eyes are subject, the Wakeful Eye that preserveth Israel, as it is written, " The Eye of the Lord is upon them that fear Him, and upon them that trust in His Goodness."

By this Most High Eye, I adjure you all evil eyes to depart and be eradicated and to flee away to a distance from the Wearer of this Amulet, and that

*you are to have no power whatever over her who
wears this Charm. And by the power of this most
Holy Seal, you shall have no authority to hurt
either by day or by night, when asleep or when
awake: nor over any of her two hundred and
forty-eight limbs, nor over any of her three hundred and sixty-five veins henceforth and for ever.
A.N.S.V.UZAH. ADIAH. LEHABIEL.*
(Hanauer 319)

A.N.S.V. is an abbreviation for 'Amen, Netzach, Tsilol, Ve'ad,
while UZAH. ADIAH. LEHABIEL are acrostics for many holy
names.

*The angel names at the end parallel the Shad-
owhunters' invocation of a particular angel when
they draw an angelic blade. The letter combina-
tions before this, often formed from the names of
angels, were added to these amulets and scrolls –
The letters' position would power the charms and
protect the wearer.*
(Hanauer 320)

*Letters are sacred in Judaism, as they are believed
to be crafted by God. There's a tradition of magic
using Hebrew letters: Golems are brought to life
(in folklore) by inscribing Hebrew letters on them.
In the tradition of the Kabbalah, the Mark of Cain
was likely a Hebrew letter written by God. In fact,
the Zohar, mystical book of Kabbalah, describes*

*major significances of each Hebrew letter, from
God creating the world with a Bet (for Berisheet,
in the beginning, the first world of the Bible and of
creation) to Alef, the silent letter that begins the
Hebrew alphabet and encompasses everything.*
(Frankel)

3

Lexicon of the More Famous Angels

There are "seventy names of angels which are good for protection against all sorts of dangers" (Trachtenberg 98). Their names are usually concocted of a root indicating the specific function they perform, and a suffix meaning "God," usually "el." Shadowhunters are advised to consider the angel they most wish to invoke when naming their blades, as it's believed that each particular angel invoked with bring part of its own spirit to the blade. Each has valuable gifts to bring to particular situations. It is said, with a truly desperate prayer for help, one should use an angel who particularly carries messages to God's throne: Michael, Raphael, Metatron, Abuliel, or Sandalphon.

Abrariel

In ceremonial magic tracts, an angel used for invoking emotions, who is called upon in fertility and birth rituals. He is one of the regents of the moon. Jace invokes him while awaiting Magnus for other rituals, before they charge into battle against Valentine and his forces of fear and death in *City of Ashes*.

Amriel or Ambriel

This angel inspires clear communication and is an angel of general protection. He is the special protector of those with the sign of Gemini born in the month of May. He aids people to find new jobs and opportunities and repels negative energies. Alec draws the blade Amriel, intending to attack Camille but finds Maureen instead – clear understanding and communication are needed here indeed.

Anael

"Grace of God." Prince of the Archangels and ruler of the Friday angels, as well as one of the seven angels of creation and Lord of the planet Venus. Angel of students, teachers, and learning, who can be invoked for help with romance, harmony, self-confidence, and inner peace. He helps people with creative pursuits and creates beauty wherever he goes. Will names his blade this battling Mrs. Dark in *Clockwork Angel*, suggesting love to fight the evil matriarch.

Arathiel

In the Silent City, Alec names his blade this after the angel of the first hour of the night (*City of Ashes*). This seems fitting. Arathiel means "The earth of God."

Ariel

Ariel's name means "Lion of God." As the patron angel of wild animals, he heals and protects nature. He also helps people achieve goals and is a glorious golden angel of fire.

Azrael, Izrail

"Whom God helps." God's most faithful servant. He was the one who succeeded in collecting earth to make Adam, so God decreed he would bring death to men in the end. Azrael helps people cross over to heaven at the time of death, so those on earth call upon Azrael for support and comfort.

Camael

Chief of the Order of Powers, Camael ("One who sees God") is the personification of divine justice among the seven angels that stand in the presence of God. He presides over self-discipline, beauty, joy, happiness, power in interpersonal relationships, and contentment. The classic Essene prayer says: "Camael, Angel of Joy, descend upon the earth and give beauty to all things." In fact, Jace invokes him while awaiting Magnus, who can offer additional gifts, in *City of Ashes*.

Cassiel

Ruler of Saturday. Cassiel is one of the Sarim (princes) of the Order of Powers. Sometimes, he appears as the angel of temperance. This angel of solitude and tears teaches patience and helps people overcome long term problems. Nonetheless, the "Speed of God" generally watches over earth without interfering. Jace encourages Clary to summon him as they find all of Idris under demon attack – but also tells her to stay out of the fighting as much as she can.

Chamuel

"He who seeks God." Chamuel is a powerful healer and leader of the Powers or Dominions. He may also be the shadowy angel of the Bible who wrestled with Jacob all night. He is the healer of relationships, helping seekers find inner peace and the power to forgive. Call upon Chamuel for comfort, protection, and finding what's been lost.

Dumah

The angel of silence and death's stillness. The Angel of Death brings him the souls of those who are gone, for him to sort into the righteous and unrighteous. There's a late Midrashic statement that each day at eventide Dumah releases the spirits in his charge during their first year to travel, eat, and drink. "Therefore, whoever drinks water at twilight robs his dead." He is the guardian angel of Egypt, the angel of silence and punishment. Appropriately, Sebastian invokes this angel of death in *City of Lost Souls* to kill the demon who double-crosses him (287).

Eremiel

Will calls on this angel "He Will Obtain God's Mercy" when rescuing Tatiana from the demon worm. A great angel who presides over the Abyss and Hades, Eremiel watches over souls in the underworld. In the Apocalypse of Zephaniah, he assists in judgment, the same function Will serves in this scene.

Gabriel

Gabriel's name means "God is my strength." Gabriel is the angel of art and communication. He is also a warrior and offerer of purification and patron saint of messengers. Call on him to purify your thoughts and feelings, as well as your body. Jace calls on him when the Fairie Court proves themselves treacherous – a deadly threat, as he's surrounded.

Jibreel, as he's known in Islam, brought the Qur'an to Prophet Muhammad. He's called Mighty in Power as well as *Dhoo Mirrah* (free from any defect in body and mind and possessing a beautiful appearance) (Qur'an 53:5-6). The Hadiths also describe Jibreel in detail:

> *The Messenger of Allah said, describing Jibreel: 'I saw Jibreel descending from heaven, and his great size filled the space between heaven and earth' (…) The Messenger of Allah saw Jibreel in his true form. He had six hundred wings, each of which covered the horizon. There fell from his wings jewels, pearls and rubies, only Allah knows about*

them.
(Hadith)

Haniel

"Glory of God" Haniel is a ruler in the order of Principalities and a ruler of Venus. Call upon Haniel to find beauty, harmony, natural healing, and grace.

Harahel

Harahel "all knowing God" holds dominion over libraries, archives, schools and universities. He opens us to new ideas and inspires us to use knowledge to benefit others. Nonetheless, he's used to imprison Jace in *City of Ashes,* symbolizing knowledge and the law turning against the young Shadowhunter.

Israfel, Israfiel

This angel is "the burning one" from the Koran. Reigning over music, hope, and inspiration, he blows the trumpet of God and has the sweetest voice of any angel. It's said he kept Mohammad company for three years. Jace invokes him to fight Raum demons in *City of Ashes* and Will uses this blade to fight Mrs. Dark, linking the characters.

Ithuriel

Ithuriel, discovery of God, carries a spear that burns away false images. His gift is revealing the truth to those who seek it. "I know he's an angel with the worst luck in the world….Angels have different dominions of power, and his is protection," Clare notes, explaining how she came to use him in *Clockwork Princess* as well as *City of Glass* (*Cassandra Clare's Clockwork Princess Bus Tour*). In *Paradise Lost*, Ithuriel appears – he's Eve's guardian who wakes her before Satan can whisper lies to her:

> *Ithuriel and Zephon, with winged speed*
> *Search through this garden; leave unsearched no nook;*
> *But chiefly where those two fair creatures lodge,*
> *Now laid perhaps asleep, secure of harm.*
> *(…)*
> *Him [i.e. Satan], thus intent Ithuriel with his spear*
> *Touched lightly; for no falsehood can endure*
> *Touch of celestial temper, but returns*
> *Of force to its own likeness.*
> (IV:788-791, 810-813)

Ithuriel reveals hidden characteristics and helps people harness their dreams, intuition, and innate talents (Davidson). He's also mentioned in the poem "The Hour of the Angel" by Rudyard Kipling, which describes the final judgment as "Ithuriel's Hour." Under his influence, Tessa and Clary both reach inside themselves to reveal true inner power to save the entire world of Shadowhunters. Using "the sum of all [their] past" – their experiences and lessons – they do indeed find "victory at the last."

The Hour of the Angel

Sooner or late – in earnest or in jest –
(But the stakes are no jest) Ithuriel's Hour
Will spring on us, for the first time, the test
Of our sole unbacked competence and power
Up to the limit of our years and dower
Of judgment – or beyond. But here we have
Prepared long since our garland or our grave.

For, at that hour, the sum of all our past,
Act, habit, thought, and passion, shall be cast
In one addition, be it more or less,
And as that reading runs so shall we do;
Meeting, astounded, victory at the last,
Or, first and last, our own unworthiness.
And none can change us though they die to save!
(743)

Jahoel

Mediator of the ineffable name; prince of the presence and chief of the Seraphim. He's a guardian of musicians and singers and leads the choir that sings God's praises. Jace calls on him as they find all of Idris under demon attack.

Jeremiel

"Mercy of God" He's an archangel of prophetic visions and helps newly-crossed over souls to review their lives just as he helps those on earth to take inventory of their lives. A guide to visions, life review and psychic dreams, he's mentioned in the *Book of Enoch.* Will draws on this in the Sanctuary in *Clockwork Angel,* praying that his Tessa is still alive.

Jophiel

Jophiel's name means "Beauty of God." He is said to have guarded the tree of knowledge and expelled Adam and Eve. Jophiel helps us to think beautiful thoughts and to therefore create, manifest, and attract more beauty into our lives. The patron angel of artists and those embarking on creative projects, he helps us channel illumination and perception. At the same time, some believe him to be the angel who threw Adam and Eve out of paradise – appropriately, his name is used to imprison Jace in *City of Ashes.*

Malik, Malichai

While not precisely the name of an angel, this is the generic term for angel or messenger. In the Islamic tradition, Malik, whose name literally means "Master," is the Keeper of Hell, as Allah says: "They (the people in Hell) will cry: 'O Malik! Would that your Lord put an end to us!'..." (Qur'an 43:77). Malik tells the denizens of hell that they must remain there forever because "they abhorred the truth when [it] was brought to them." As Mrs. Black attacks in *Clockwork Angel*, Will names his blade Malik, banishing her from the world of the righteous.

Metatron

Metatron is found in early Jewish mystical texts. He is the angel who stands behind God's throne and performs miracles on his behalf. As God's secretary, he is the angel of mankind and almost as large as the world. With a name that's the mathematical equivalent of Shaddai, one of God's names, he can be seen as a stand-in. He protects those below, especially small children with special gifts. In one tale, gazing into the burning bush caused Moses to have visions:

> *Hereupon God commanded Metatron, the Angel*
> *of the Face, to conduct Moses to the celestial*
> *regions amid the sound of music and song, and He*
> *commanded him furthermore to summon thirty*
> *thousand angels, to serve as his body-guard, fif-*
> *teen thousand to right of him and fifteen thou-*
> *sand to left of him. In abject terror Moses asked*
> *Metatron, "Who art thou?" and the angel replied,*
> *"I am Enoch, the son of Jared, thy ancestor, and*
> *God has charged me to accompany thee to His*
> *throne."*
> (Ginzburg "The Ascension of Moses")

Michael

"Who is like God?" His name is said to be a battle cry. He is the angel of fearlessness, who gives guidance and direction. Field Commander of the Lord's Host and leader of the Archangels, he is the angel of protection, justice and strength. He controls natural phenomena like rain, wind, and clouds, and provides protection, courage, power and strength. In art, he's always portrayed with a sword or lance, often in battle with the devil. He was the one to hurl Satan out of heaven. Thus Jace names his blade this to fight Lilith herself in *City of Fallen Angels*.

> *And at that time shall Michael stand up, the great prince which standeth for the children of thy people: and there shall be a time of trouble, such as never was since there was a nation even to that same time: and at that time thy people shall be delivered, every one that shall be found written in the book.*
> (Daniel 12.1)

Nakir

According to the Islamic tradition, the angels Nakir and Munkir question the person in the grave. They are blue-black and visit the tombs of the recently dead and question them to determine whether they will go to paradise or to hell. Jace calls on them when demon-fighting in *City of Ashes*, then hands Nakir to Clary. Likewise, Will names his blade thus in *Clock-*

work *Princess* as a character link between himself and Jace. Clary calls her blade this fighting Elapid demons during *City of Lost Souls,* and *Heavenly Fire* sees Jace call his blade this again – a personal favorite, it seems.

Nuriel

Alec names his blade this when battling Camille in *Lost Souls.* He's the angel of control and physical power over others. He is sometimes called the angel of fire, as his name derives from that word. Thus vampires, who are masters of control, yet vulnerable to fire, may have a weakness to this angel and his domain.

> *In the second heaven Moses saw the angel Nuriel, standing three hundred parasangs high, with his retinue of fifty myriads of angels, all fashioned out of water and fire...these were the angels set over the clouds, the winds, and the rains, who return speedily, as soon as they have executed the will of their Creator, to their station in the second of the heavens, there to proclaim the praise of God.* (Ginzburg "The Ascension of Moses" *The Legends of the Jews*)

Phanuel

Phanuel "The Face of God" is ruler of the Ophanim, the fourth angel who stands before God in the *Book of Enoch,* after Michael, Raphael, and Gabriel. His was one of the four voices Enoch heard praising God.

> *This first is Michael, the merciful and long-suffering: and the second, who is set over all the diseases and all the wounds of the children of men, is Raphael: and the third, who is set over all the powers, is Gabriel: and the fourth, who is set over the repentance unto hope of those who inherit eternal life, is named Phanuel.*
> (1 Enoch 40:9)

Raguel

"Friend of God." The angel of penance reaches out to his brethren and makes sure they're working in harmony. Call upon him in situations requiring trust and fellowship.

Raphael

"God heals." As well as bringing physical healing, he is the angel of love and laughter, a guardian of science, communication, and young people. He defeated the demon Azazel and protected mundanes from the schemes of Asmodeus. He brings healing to body, mind, and spirit and in particular protects against poison and heals the earth. In Edom, Magnus tells Alec to name his blade in honor of their vampire friend, who maintained faith in God all his life.

Raziel

"Each day the angel Raziel makes proclamations on Mount Horeb, from heaven, of the secrets of men to all that dwell upon the earth, and his voice resounds throughout the world," explains *Targum Ecclesiastes*, a collection of explanatory stories about the Book of Ecclesiastes (10:20).

Raziel's name means "secret of God" because of the special wisdom God grants him. Originally, Raziel taught the Shadowhunters all the runes through his magical Book and brought them the Mortal Instruments. When he shows himself, he is covered in Nephilim runes, but gold and living ones, with golden wings and an eye set in each feather (*City of Glass* 491). He is the angel of answers to unponderable questions, guardian of original thinkers. (Out of respect, Shadowhunters do not invoke Raziel.)

Samandiriel

This angel inspires imagination and helps to invoke creativity at need. He's also an angel of fertility.

Sandalphon

Sandalphon's name means "brother" in Greek, a reference to his twin, Metatron. The twins are the only archangels who were originally mortal men, for it's said he was once the prophet Elijah. The two brothers weave prayers into wreathes for God to wear. Sandalphon is "taller than his comrades by a distance of five hundred years," but his significance lies in his intimate attendance upon God Himself. Sandalphon's chief role is to carry human prayers to God, so they may be answered. He is the patron angel of music. While his name is used to imprison Jace, Alec also invokes it in *Fallen Angels* as they explore the cult of Lilith and defeat it with human strength and courage.

Seraphiel

This eagle-headed angel and leader of the Seraphim punishes those who defy God's will. He provides contentment and peace of mind. The angel of silence.

Sanvi, Sansanvi and Semangelo

In legend, these were the angels God sent against Lilith to force her to return to Eden. Thus, these names are a charm against her and were often placed in the corners of a house to protect children against the hazards of infancy. Jace invokes them when he visits Clary's house as her new protector in the first book.

Tahariel

An angel of purity who cleanses thoughts, spirits or surroundings. He offers a respite from everyday relationships and a connection to a higher spirituality. Appropriately, he's used to imprison Jace in *City of Ashes*.

Telantes

An angel invoked in the Solomanic Grimoires, likewise invoked by Jace in *City of Ashes* as they wait for the sorcerous Magnus.

Uriel

Uriel "Light of God" is the angel of wisdom and logical thought. In Judaism, he's often viewed as the angel of repentance – in fact, Jewish tradition says that Uriel wielded a fiery sword to guard the gates of the Garden of Eden after Adam and Eve sinned. The classic *Paradise Lost* portrays Uriel as "the sharpest sighted spirit in all of heaven" who also watches over a great ball of light: the sun. He also illuminates situations and gives prophetic information and warnings. Angel of nature, visions and instruction and the custodian of prophecy. A patron angel of literature and music. Uriel is considered an archangel who helps us with natural disaster. One should call upon Archangel Uriel to avert such events, or to heal and recover in their aftermath. Will names his blade this when first battling the Dark Sisters.

Zadkiel

"Righteousness of God" He is the ruler of Jupiter and chief of the Dominions. He is also the angel of divine justice. He is the angel of invocation and transformation, as well as freedom, benevolence, tolerance, and mercy. The patron angel of all who forgive.

4

The Nature of Demons

Asmodeus explains in *City of Heavenly Fire*: "To be an artist of pain, to create agony, to blacken the soul, to turn pure motives to filth and love to lust and then to hate, to turn a source of joy to a source of torture, *that* is what we exist for!" (633). Demons represent ultimate greed and destruction – a desire to toy with the world or invade it and burn it down. To demons, people are playthings to be tortured because their loves and fears make them vulnerable. The creatures live on mankind's pain and suffering, from the cries of those doomed to hell to memories and emotions. Thomas Aquinas explains:

> *The assault itself is due to the malice of the*
> *demons, who through envy endeavor to hinder*
> *man's progress; and through pride usurp a sem-*
> *blance of Divine power, by deputing certain minis-*
> *ters to assail man, as the angels of God in their*
> *various offices minister to man's salvation.*
> (Aquinas 114.1)

Demon, derived from the word *daio* "to divide" originally applied to gods, emphasizing their separate nature from man. Certainly, many demons are ex-gods (not just the fallen angels, but the many gods of a prior or competing religion in many places of the world). They're all over the world, in their different forms – Greek daemons, Persian daevas, Hindu asuras, Japanese oni (*Codex* 57). In Islam the evil jinns are referred to as the shayātīn, or devils, while Buddhism has hells peopled by demons that represent mental obstructions. Most belief systems have some method of incorporating both their existence and the fight against them. Shadowhunters cleave to no single religion, and in turn all religions assist them in their battle. As he tells Clary after gathering weapons hidden in the church, "I could as easily have gone for help to a Jewish synagogue or a Shinto temple." Clare adds:

> *I wanted to make sure multiple types of demonic myth were present, not just the Christian view of them, so you'll find Japanese, Indian, Tibetan, and other kinds of demons represented (plus the kind I've made up.) I read a lot of old "demonologies" – there was a whole time period where scholars were obsessed with listing every kind of demon and mapping Hell.*
> ("Interview: Cassandra Clare")

To Christians the greatest force of evil is the Devil, often equated with fallen angel Lucifer or Satan, the adversary angel who challenges God in the Book of Job. The Fourth Lateran Council issued the decree: "Diabolus enim et alii daemones" (the devil and the other demons), i.e. the chief of the demons is called the devil. Satan is clearly included among the daemons in James 2:19 and in Luke 11:15-18. "For our wrestling is not against flesh and blood; but against principalities and powers, against the rulers of the world of this darkness, against the spirits of wickedness in the high places" (Ephesians 6:12). Saint Thomas Aquinas declares in Summa Theologica 50.5:

> **Objection 1.** *It would seem that the angels are not incorruptible; for Damascene, speaking of the angel, says (De Fide Orth. ii, 3) that he is "an intellectual substance, partaking of immortality by favor, and not by nature."*

> **Objection 2.** *Further, Plato says in the Timaeus: "O gods of gods, whose maker and father am I: You are indeed my works, dissoluble by nature, yet indissoluble because I so will it." But gods such as these can only be understood to be the angels. Therefore the angels are corruptible by their nature*

> **Objection 3.** *Further, according to Gregory (Moral. xvi), "all things would tend towards nothing, unless the hand of the Almighty preserved them." But what can be brought to nothing is corruptible. Therefore, since the angels were made by God, it would appear that they are corruptible of their own nature.*

Aquinas, however, believes they are incorruptible because of the matter that makes them up. Nonetheless, he sees Lucifer as a fallen angel: In this way the angel sinned, by seeking his own good, from his own free-will, insubordinately to the rule of the Divine will (Aquinas 63.1). He quotes Isaiah 14:12: "How art thou fallen … O Lucifer, who didst rise in the morning!"

Lucifer, whose name means "light bearer" in Latin, rebelled against God and then became Satan, the leader of the fallen angels. When Lucifer fell from heaven, it was "like lightning," says Luke 10:18, and he shone like a falling star (Lucifer is associated with Venus, the star of the morning). The Bible warns in 2 Corinthians 11:14 that "Satan himself masquerades as an angel of light." Fallen angels are filled with anguish, for they once beheld the light of God and never will again. According to Augustine (De Civ. Dei xii, 1): "There are two cities, that is, two societies, one of the good angels and men, the other of the wicked."

Judaism has no devil, but folklore and superstition introduce another presence besides God and his angels. Enoch 36:1 describes angels, spirits, and men, emphasizing another force at play in the world. In Jewish legend, demons were forces opposed to mankind, most likely the children of Lilith.

> *Talmudic Jewry owned a highly elaborated demonology, distinguishing between classes and even individuals, with a wealth of detail concerning the nature and pursuits of the evil spirits. Its elements grew naturally out of the fertile popular imagination, convinced as it was of the reality of the spirit world, and fortified by a rich tradition drawn largely from the folklores of Egypt and Babylon and Persia. This lore served a dual need:*

it conveyed the power of control, and at the same time of self-protection.
(Trachtenberg 25)

Most of the study was spent in determining forms of protection.

During her introduction to demons in *City of Bones,* Jace tells Clary: "That's not a person, little girl. It may look like a person and talk like a person and maybe even bleed like a person. But it's a monster." As Jace adds:

It's not the same thing at all. Vampires, werewolves, even warlocks, they're part-human. Part of this world, born in it. They belong here. But demons come from other worlds. They're interdimensional parasites. They come to a world and use it up. They can't build, just destroy – they can't make, only use. They drain a place to ashes and when it's dead, they move on to the next one. It's life they want-not just your life or mine, but all the life of this world, its rivers and cities, its oceans, its everything. And the only thing that stands between them and the destruction of all this" – he pointed outside the window of the carriage, waving his hand as if he meant to indicate everything in the city from the skyscrapers uptown to the clog of traffic on Houston Street – "is the Nephilim."
(*City of Bones*)

Greater Demons live in the great Void between worlds, though they can be summoned to earth through Warlocks' pentagrams. When they are killed on earth, they are actually banished to the void, there to reform over centuries. Lesser demons, however, can be killed on earth. Clare adds:

> *Demons are, in some form, living creatures. As such, they are vulnerable to physical accidents. If a (flightless) demon falls off a high cliff, they won't survive even though the ground wasn't runed. If a (exoskeleton-free) demon gets buried in a rock-slide, they won't survive even though the rocks weren't runed. The same goes for getting crushed under large objects, like chandeliers, grand pianos, and roof collapses. I'm sure that at one or another point in history, Shadowhunters put runes all over trebuchets, catapults, and their ammunition. Did they need to? Probably not, but it couldn't hurt.*
> (Clare Tumblr, July 2015)

The Hagigah (a tractate of the Babylonian Talmud or Bible commentary) describes demons thusly: "Six things have been said about demons: Like angels they have wings, and are able to fly from one end of the world to another, and know the future. Like men, the demons take nourishment, marry, beget children, and ultimately die." *The Shadowhunters Codex* and the series offer a bit more.

Demon energy, a life-giving spark, keeps them alive in the human dimension. When demons die, this energy is separated from its physical body and will return to its home dimension, Hell. When some, especially Greater Demons, die, they are shattered into pieces and scattered in between worlds, taking them centuries to reform. Demons have blood of a sort with greenish black ichor, as opposed to the golden blood of angels. This ichor is somewhat toxic and can burn what it touches. There are a number of demon languages that the Nephilim have identified, including Chthonic, Purgatic, Gehennic and Tartarian. (These words reference names for Hell – Purgatory, Gehenna, and Tartarus. "Chthonic" means "relating to the Underworld.)

> *One Jewish source related that the demons were created on the Sixth Day of Creation when the Lord was producing many creatures, but He was interrupted by the approaching eve of Sabbath, and so there was not enough time to give all the souls He had created bodies of their own. Another Jewish source claimed that a demon race existed long before humankind and grew so arrogant that finally humans were created to replace them. They were left hanging about in resentful droves. The notion of the demon as an elder sibling/spirit who came before humankind is found in the folk-lore and myth of many traditions. It is said to explain their attitude and their sense of prior claim on property, thus expecting tithes or sacrifices from mortal usurpers.*
> *(Mack XXXIV)*

Clare's demons can sometimes produce Hellmist, "a sort of enchanted demonic smoke" that mutes the effects of some magic, used during a demon attack in *City of Glass* as the team portal to Idris (24). There are also the mysterious demonic runes. Clare adds:

> *No one knows who created demonic runes any*
> *more than anyone knows who created demons or,*
> *for that matter, who created English. (In fact, we*
> *know there are multiple demonic languages, each*
> *presumably with its own runes.) Demonic magic*
> *is a chaotic, varied, complicated thing that doesn't*
> *make a lot of sense to humans; what partial*
> *knowledge warlocks have managed to figure out*
> *about it and how to use it is, exactly, what the Spi-*
> *ral Labyrinth and things like the Book of the*
> *White contain.*
> (Clare Tumblr, Feb 2015)

In legends around the world, there are always telltale signs to reveal a demon isn't truly human: some demons don't cast a shadow, or always have wet shirt hems. Some demons are unfinished, with missing backs or tops to their heads. Some have backwards legs. Even when at a village dance, it can always be recognized by its feet: whether they are those of a rooster, goat, goose, or pig, webbed, or a fish's tail, a discreet glance down will confirm its true nature.

While some can speak, demons lack reason, love, and compassion. Further, most demons are doomed to vanish at dawn. Human legends describe people outwitting the creatures or escaping through holy protections if they wish to preserve themselves and the ones they love.

> *Many of the most powerful demons can be as easily tricked as little children because, although supernatural, they lack the intelligence of angels or the human's potential ability to think logically or gain wisdom. They also lack the human ability to rationalize or justification. They simply are. They are also quite literally heartless and love is so alien it can melt them.*
>
> (Mack xv)

5

Protections

Jewish Magic and Superstition by Joshua Trachtenberg explains several ways to protect oneself from demons according to ancient beliefs.

> *Light was one of these protective agents, due, no doubt, to the circumstance that demons shun the light, and also because of the purificatory and expiatory virtues of fire, the source of light. In the Talmud we read that "carrying a torch at night is as good as having a companion (to keep the demons away), while walking by moonlight is equivalent to having two companions."*

Sefer Hasidim advises that "anyone who is threatened by demons and approaches fire before uttering a word about it, will not be harmed nor die." This reliance on light explains the commonness of light at religious ceremonies and holidays to ward off the forces of evil.

Like fire, water is a potent cleanser. Across the world, the natural barrier of running water is said to protect man from fairies, demons, witches, and so on. Trachtenberg writes: "Running water neutralizes a magic act, and destroys the magical properties of things; it dispels mirages created by demons, and drives off the spirits themselves" (159). People would even spit to ward off evil with a part of themselves.

Clattering sounds were another demon repellent, with people shaking stones in a jar or shouting. "Ringing of church bells have the same effect; on the *Polterabend*, preceding a wedding, the demons that threatened bride and groom were driven off by setting up a great clamor and breaking pottery" (Trachtenberg 160). Sunlight can frighten off or kill dark forces – as Simon demonstrates in the first book.

The Shadowhunters have wards – "a sort of magical fence system" which the first generation of Shadowhunters established around the earth. They keep many of the demons out and are centered over Wrangel Island. However, they are weakening through *Lost Souls* and *Heavenly Fire*. Presumably, this will be solved in the next series.

Cold iron was also traditional. Forged iron was a hallmark of civilization, a way to set man apart from the natural world, "and thus evidently antipathetic to the spirit masters of primitive pre-metal society" (Trachtenberg 162).

Will Herondale describes the London Institute as protected by more than the blood of Shadowhunters: "Every beam is carved of rowan wood. Every nail used to hammer the beams together is made of silver, iron, or electrum. The place is built on hallowed ground surrounded by wards" *(Clockwork Angel* 91). Likewise, Isabelle wears a gold anklet to protect herself from demons and Valentine has electrum-plated braces. The Codex describes gold as having positive and negative associations in religion – it is beautiful and resistant to corruption but also a source of greed. Electrum is called "a good conductor of magic" (25). The Silent Brothers experiment on Jace's heavenly fire with gold, silver, steel, and rowan wood (*Heavenly Fire* 229). Jace enters a church in the first book and discovers "Vials of holy water, blessed knives, steel and silver blades…electrum wire – not much use at the moment, but it's always good to have spare – silver bullets, charms of protection, crucifixes, stars of David."

The church's protection against demons and fairies is well known in European folklore. Holy water, crucifixes, and blessed weapons are popular in battles against demons as well as vampires. The series, of course, emphasizes the power of all holy symbols, across religions.

Silver is a metal of purity. The Incas, the Chinese, the Europeans, and the Egyptians all used silver amulets to protect oneself from evil. While gold had sun power, silver meant the moon as well as purity (explaining its strength against werewolves). Due to its reflective properties, silver could reveal the truth or catch the light and repel the darkness. It actually has some antimicrobial properties that ancient people noticed as water in a silver pitcher stayed clear longer than in other containers. Electrum (the natural alloy of gold and silver) was used in jewelry by the Egyptians from 5000 BCE. They called it white gold, attributing many qualities of silver to it.

Rowan wood is likewise protective with red berries like drops of blood with visible five pointed stars imprinted there. Its white blossoms marked it as a fairy tree. In Greek myth, an eagle's blood, fallen to earth in a battle with demons, created the plant. The Norse used its wood for rune staves. The British especially wore it, from rowan equal-armed crosses on the lintels or sewn into coat linings to protect the wearers.

Salt was another such substance which figured prominently in the folklore of European peoples. Thus it was believed that salt is never found at the witches' Sabbat feast, and the Inquisitor and his assistants at a witch-trial were warned to wear bags containing consecrated salt for protection against the accused. Jewish folklore credited salt with an equally high potency. In Ezek. 16:4 we learn that new-born babes were rubbed with salt, a practice still current in the Orient. According to medieval authorities, salt must be set on a table before a meal is begun "because it protects one against Satan's denunciations." The Kabbalists were more outspoken: "It drives off the spirits," they wrote, "because it is the mathematical equiv-alent of three yhvh's; therefore one should dip the piece of bread over which the benediction is recited, three times into salt." "After each meal eat some salt and you will not be harmed." For this reason salt was used in many rites connected with birth, marriage and death, and in medicine. (Trachtenberg 162)

The Shadowhunters series emphasizes that children must have a ceremony performed by an Iron Sister and Silent Brother to be protected in their vulnerable childhoods. Tessa's mother, specifically, is a Shadowhunter child with no marks and no protection, who is assaulted by a demon later in life.

This emphasis on childhood vulnerability and protection is another worldwide belief.

Jewish Magic and Superstition explains that as early as the fourteenth century the ceremony called Hollekreisch was performed by many Jews in Germany. The baby was lifted into the air three times, and each time his new name was shouted out by the guests in unison with a particular formula.

> *Holle was the demon-witch who attacked infants; in this respect she provided a close parallel to the familiar Lilit. The further correspondences between the two: their connection with the night; the distinguishing physical feature, long hair, which they had in common; their propensity to attack prior to the naming of the child; all of these made the identification of the two a natural one. Shouting the child's name, which is mentioned in all the references to the ceremony, and tossing the infant in the air three times, were devices intended to drive off the demon Holle, and her fellows, just as in the Wachnacht ceremony on the night before the circumcision measures were taken to ward off attacks by Lilit.*
> (Trachtenberg 43)

Lilith amulets were popular among Jews of the Middle Ages, all designed to ward off her influence and protect the innocent, especially babies.

Pentagrams

The Pentagram, is the "doorway" for the Demon through which it will enter this world if given a right Sacrifice. It's worth remembering that pentagrams ward in all directions…except, technically, up. The origin is not well known, but the most common theory is that the stub is a flawed Star of David. The Pentagram ("five lines") is the shape of a five-pointed star drawn with five straight strokes. In Christian occult tradition the Pentagram is usually placed upside down, but that is not necessary. Based on numerology, the five points means the pentagram symbolizes the Earth element and can be used as an Earth symbol on an altar.

Ancient Greece and Babylonia had symbolic pictograms, dating back to 3000 B.C. In ancient Sumerian they're a symbol for hole or small room – where a demon must be imprisoned. It has associations with Christianity for Christ's five wounds, but also the goddess Venus and thus its other name – the morning star – Lucifer.

A summoning pentagram or five-pointed star is traditionally drawn within a circle within a square. In Lilith's church, Clary finds one that's "two concentric circles with a square in the center of them" She thinks that "The circles were meant to draw down and concentrate magical power" (*Fallen Angels* 216). The *Goetia* and the *Book of Abramelin* offered techniques for summoning and containing demons. These practitioners do not necessarily worship demons (known as "demonolatry"), but seek to deploy them to obtain their goals. The ancient spellbook the *Lesser Key of Solomon* describes the ranks of demons and instructions to summon them. Words of conjuration also appear, explaining how, in the Bible, Solomon conjured a host of demons to build his temple:

> *Beralanensis, Baldachiensis, Paumachia, and Apologia Sedes, by the most mighty kings and powers, and the most powerful princes, genii, Liachidæ, ministers of the Tartarean seat, chief prince of the seat of Apologia, in the ninth legion, I invoke you, and by invocating, conjure you; and being armed with power from the supreme Majesty, I strongly command you, by Him who spoke and it was done, and to whom all creatures are obedient; and by this ineffable name, Tetragrammaton Jehovah, which being heard the elements are overthrown, the air is shaken, the sea runneth back, the fire is quenched, the earth trembles, and all the host of the celestials, and terrestrials, and infernals do tremble together, and are troubled and confounded: wherefore, forthwith and without delay, do you come from all parts of the world, and make rational answers unto all things I shall ask of you; and come ye peaceably, visibly and affably now, without delay, manifesting what we desire, being conjured by the name of the living and true God, Helioren, and fulfill our commands, and persist unto the end, and according to our intentions, visibly and affably speaking unto us with a clear voice, intelligible, and without any ambiguity.*
> ("Of the Art Goetia")

Connected to these are ley lines. Magnus describes the Seven Sacred Sites – places in the world where ley lines converge that Warlocks use for great spells. One is a stone tomb at Poll na mBrón called "the cavern of sorrows" (*Lost Souls* 441). These energy lines exist around the world, known as "Holy Lines" to the Germans, "Dragon Lines" to the Chinese, "Spirit Lines" to Incas and Mayans, and "Song Paths" to the Australian Aborigines. While some assume the straight roads marking many of these were built by Romans, the Romans in fact record discovering them in Europe, North Africa, Crete, and Babylon. Thus they appear to be Neolithic. In his *The Fairy- Faith in Celtic Countries,* W. Y. Evans-Wentz calls them "fairy paths" or "fairy passes" of Ireland—"actual magnetic arteries, so to speak, through which circulates the earth's magnetism" (33).

The term "ley lines" comes from amateur archaeologist Alfred Watkins with his book 1921 book *The Old Straight Track,* which popularized the term. He charted standing stones, long-barrows, cairns, dolmens, mounds, mark-stones, stone circles, henges, springs, fords, wells, castles, beacon-hills, churches, crossroads, and hill-forts, only to find they were laid out in straight lines, with hills as start (or finish) point (4). Often ley lines are constructed to match astronomical events: One of the largest in England, St. Michael's Ley, is aligned along the path of the sun on the 8th of May – St. Michael's Day. This line passes through several megalithic sites, then reaches Glastonbury, the artificial hill or former island famed from Arthurian legend, and then on to the stone circle at Avebury, all the way to the town of Penzance on the coast.

6

Holy Symbols

And it came to pass, when Joshua was by Jericho, that he lifted up his eyes and looked, and, behold, there stood a man over against him with his sword drawn in his hand: and Joshua went unto him, and said unto him, Art thou for us, or for our adversaries? And he said, Nay; but as captain of the host of the LORD am I now come. And Joshua fell on his face to the earth, and did worship, and said unto him, What saith my lord unto his servant? And the captain of the LORD'S host said unto Joshua, Loose thy shoe from off thy foot; for the place whereon thou standest is holy. And Joshua did so.
(Joshua 5:13-15)

As captain of the host, this is assumed to be the Archangel Michael. He gave Joshua his own sword, and with it, Joshua led his army against Jericho. By God's blessing, the walls fell, and Joshua captured the city. Michael and the other angels are soldiers, often armed for battle. Simon is given this very sword in *City of Lost Souls*, to separate Jace from Sebastian with Heaven's fire.

The Clave inscribe the Seal of Solomon on Simon's cell door in *City of Glass*. His Jewish mother protects herself with religious symbols (the Star of David, Chai, and hamsa), and on the doorknob, she puts tefillin, a leather box filled with scripture, with straps to wear it on the hand and the head.

> *Tefillin symbolize a submission to God, as well as a unity of mind and heart. Simon places his hand on the mezuzah on the doorway; commonly kept there, a mezuzah is inscribed with the Sh'ma Yisrael (" Hear, O Israel! The Lord is our God . . ."), which Simon later recites in his mind, when Raziel raises his hand to destroy him.*
> (Spencer, Kindle Locations 1887-1892)

Yet all the time, the Shadowhunters appropriate angelic weapons, used in their battle against the darkness. Angelic weapons marked with runes are powerful against demons because they stop demons from instantly healing. Other holy symbols – crosses and holy water but nonChristian symbols as well – are used to stop the vampires, fair folk, demons and other threats. There are many other holy weapons historically and mythically used around the world:

Angel Amulets

The Jewish tradition offers the *kimiyah* or "angel text," with names of angels or Torah passages written on parchment squares by rabbinical scribes and sealed in a silver case.

Animal Totems

Native American totems represent the family ancestors and offer protection.

Ankh

The Egyptian cross surmounted by a loop symbolizes a mythical eternal life, rebirth, and the life-giving power of the sun.

Bells

Loud, clear chimes are popular worldwide for warding off evil. In Asia, these are wind chimes, in Europe, church bells.

Bindi

In India, women wear *sindoor* or *bindi* on their forehead to protect their husband's life. Holy ash is smeared on the forehead as a protection against evil eye or ghosts.

The Buddha

In Thailand, Buddha amulets are common, though in ancient times, symbols such as conch shells or the footprints of the Buddha appeared more.

Chai

This two letter word "Hy" is the Hebrew word for life. Many Jews wear this word as a pendent for luck and protection. Its numerical value is eighteen, so the number eighteen is also sacred and protective (hence Simon's jokes about traditional $18 checks warding off vampires.)

Crucifix

In Christian tradition, this is a defense against the unholy, as the holy sign of Christ's victory over every evil.

Ekeko Amulet

In Bolivia and some places in Argentina, this god's symbol offers powerful protection when offered banknotes in turn.

Eoh

The rune *Eoh* (yew) protects against evil and harm for the ancient Scandinavians and Germanic peoples.

Evil eye

Disks or balls with concentric blue and white circles representing an evil eye are common in the Middle East. The staring eyes, ever watchful, are intended to bend the malicious gaze back to the sorcerer.

Eye of Horus or God's Eye

This diamond shape, often constructed from sticks and yarn, represents the eye of Egyptian sun-god Horus who lost an eye battling Set. A popular charm to ward off evil.

Gargoyles

In Western Europe, gargoyles (small monster statues generally on buildings) were believed to ward off evil spirits with their own grotesqueness.

Guardian Masks

In Nepal, people put Guardian Masks in their windows to ward off evil. They depict a crowned figure with a third eye who could in fact be a Shadowhunter.

Hamsa

A hand-shaped talisman against the evil eye found in the Middle East. The word means five (referring to the fingers) and a blue or green lapis eye often appears in the figure's center. In Jewish culture, the *hamsa* is sometimes called the Hand of Miriam; in some Muslim populated cultures, the Hand of Fatima.

Hexagram

This six-pointed star is the symbol of Biblical David. When surrounded by a circle, it represents the "divine mind" (a counterfeit of God's wisdom). It can also signify the unity of masculine and feminine energy. The number six represents unity and balance, specifically between man and the Divine. Aleister Crowley created his own variation, to create a symbol that could be drawn in one continuous line.

Holy Books

Jews, Christians, and Muslims have also at times used their holy books as talismans, reading them, or using the physical touch of the books.

Horseshoes

Common in Europe against fairies and devils, particularly because of the cold iron that forms them.

Italian Horn (Cornu, Cornicello, Unicorn horn, Leprechaun staff)

The ancient amulet worn in Italy as protection against "evil eye" is also linked to Celtic and Druid myths and beliefs.

Nazar

A Turkish evil eye token found in beads or on houses.

Oak

"The oak tree is often considered the 'most mundane' of woods, and from this very fact, it draws its power" (*Codex* 26). This is the wood most often used for stakes.

Omamori

This Japanese amulet dedicated to a particular saint, resembles a small envelope. It's often a brocade bag with a blessing inside. Some have a specific focus.

Pentacle

This modern symbol of Wicca is the most common Pagan symbol. The five points represent the four elements plus the spirit, and the circle around it connects them all.

Raksha

Mantras of India are inscribed on silver or gold foil and enclosed in silver cases and worn around the neck, hand or waist to protect against evil eye.

Rosaries

These strings of beads (from the Latin for crown of roses) are used to count one's prayers and symbolize a connection with Mary, Queen of Heaven.

Saint Benedict Medal

This signifies a prayer of exorcism against Satan, and a prayer for protection from temptation. Some contain the phrase "Vade Retro Satana": "Step back, Satan."

Saint Christopher Medals

These often appear hung on rearview mirrors of vehicles to invoke God's protection during travel.

Salt

This is a symbol of human domestication and purification. Since it's necessary to human life, it's believed to ward off the unclean.

Scapulars

Some Catholic Sacramentals are believed to defend against evil, thanks to their association with a specific saint or archangel. The Scapular of St. Michael the Archangel, formed of two segments of cloth, blue and black with a small shield, show the angel slaying a dragon. Pope Pius IX gave this scapular his blessing, but it was first formally approved under Pope Leo XIII.

Scarab

Symbol of the rising sun, the Egyptian sun god Chepri (or Khepera), and protection from evil in ancient Egypt.

Seal of Solomon

Jewish amulets emphasize text and names, and often incorporate the star-shaped Seal of Solomon. In alchemy, the seal represents the conscious and unconscious realms, as three points of the star point to the upper world and three to the lower (Cirlot 281). It is frequently circled with a ring of protection. Related protective circles were used across the world, from Vodou *vévés* to Pennsylvania Dutch hex signs.

Septagram

The seven pointed star is often called the Elven star or fairy star, as the number seven corresponds to the spirit realm or sometimes classical seven planets. They are sometimes labelled earth, air, fire, water, above, below and within.

Shanti shanti shanti

Jordan wears tattoos of this word meaning "peace or stillness." The words are chanted at the conclusion of particular Sanskrit prayers, called shanti mantras. "Shanti," which means "peace," is chanted three times. Just as important are the pauses or stillness between each. Saying the words invokes a spiritual frame of mind, though also a desire for peace in a general sense. Shanti is chanted thrice not for emphasis but to ward off disturbances in three distinct categories. In Sanskrit, these are referred to as adhi-daivikam, adhi-bhautikam and adhyat-mikam. These are "mental disturbances that come from God" such as natural disasters, "disturbances that come from the world" such as family arguments, "disturbances stemming from the self." Over each people have a different level of control, and the mantras help to remind of this. Jordan meditates to create peace and stillness in himself, but he also strives to remember which situations are his to control and which are not.

Shield Knot

The square shield knot is a considered symbol to ward off evil spirits in Celtic culture, bringing in the four elements as well as the spirit.

Snake

Most earth-centered or pagan cultures worshipped the serpent. It represents rebirth and regeneration (because of its molting), and often wisdom and protection against evil.

Ta'wiz

These Muslim amulets contain chosen text from the Quran, chosen for particular situations. The alkorsy (the Chair of God) verse is particularly popular.

Thor's Hammer

It is thought of as a pendant or rune offers protection against thieves in some places.

Tibetan Prayer Wheels

These rolls of thin paper printed over and over with the mantra (prayer) *Om Mani Padme Hum;* these are wound around an axel in a protective container and spun for spreading spiritual blessings and well-being.

Triple Moon

This modern pagan Goddess symbol represents the Maiden, Mother, and Crone as the waxing, full, and waning moon. It is also associated with feminine energy, mystery and psychic abilities.

7

Demon Hierarchy

During the Middle Ages, scholars divided Hell into hierarchies of demons to mirror the hierarchies of angels up above. Johann Weyer's *Pseudomonarchia Daemonum, or Hierarchy of Demons* appeared in 1577, with nobility titles granted to each demon as if they lived in his feudal society on earth. It is an Appendix to Johann Weyer's *De Praestigiis Daemonum* ("false monarchy of demons") from 1577. Of course, many of Clare's demons and greater demons, emphasized here in bold, are seen in the list. It's arguable that "Iblis demons" or "Moloch demons" are part of the demonic army that battles under the Greater Demon general of that name.

1. King Bael
2. Duke Agares
3. Prince Vassago
4. Marquis Samigina
5. **President Marbas**
6. Duke Valefor
7. Marquis Amon
8. Duke Barbatos
9. King Paimon
10. President Buer
11. Duke Gusion
12. Prince Sitri

13. King Beleth
14. Marquis Leraje
15. Duke Eligos
16. Duke Zepar
17. Count/President Botis
18. Duke Bathin
19. Duke Sallos
20. King Purson
21. **Count/President Marax**
22. Count/Prince Ipos
23. Duke Aim
24. Marquis Naberius
25. Count/President Glasya-Labolas
26. Duke Buné
27. Marquis/Count Ronové
28. Duke Berith
29. Duke Astaroth
30. Marquis Forneus
31. President Foras
32. **King Asmoday**
33. Prince/President Gäap
34. Count Furfur
35. Marquis Marchosias
36. Prince Stolas
37. Marquis Phenex
38. Count Halphas
39. **President Malphas**
40. **Count Räum**
41. Duke Focalor
42. Duke Vepar

43. Marquis Sabnock
44. **Marquis Shax**
45. King/Count Viné
46. Count Bifrons
47. Duke Vual
48. President Haagenti
49. Duke Crocell
50. Knight Furcas
51. King Balam
52. Duke Alloces
53. President Caim
54. Duke/Count Murmur
55. Prince Orobas
56. Duke Gremory
57. President Ose
58. President Amy
59. Marquis Orias
60. Duke Vapula
61. King/President Zagan
62. President Valac
63. Marquis Andras
64. Duke Haures
65. Marquis Andrealphus
66. Marquis Cimeies
67. Duke Amdusias
68. **King Belial**
69. Marquis Decarabia
70. Prince Seere
71. **Duke Dantalion**
72. Count Andromalius

8

Greater Demons

Abbadon

Inside Madame Dorothea is "A Greater Demon. Abbadon – one of the Ancients. The Lord of the Fallen" (*Bones* 361). Simon Lewis, surprisingly, is the one to slay it, by shattering a window and shining sunlight on it. He is "a nine-foot-tall rotting human skeleton" (*Codex* 67). In Revelations, Abaddon is a star who falls to Earth from heaven and is given the key to open the bottomless pit. He opens the pit, releasing a swarm of locusts. "And they had a king over them, which is the angel of the bottomless pit, whose name in the Hebrew tongue is Abaddon, but in the Greek tongue hath his name Apollyon" (Revelations 9:11). In *The Greater Key of Solomon*, Moses invokes his name to bring the plague of destructive rain down over Egypt.

> *He is the one who lets out curses to plague mankind, much as he does in the most vicious battle of the first book. He represents a challenge for the teens and a chance to see how they all fight: Alec foolishly risks himself and is nearly killed, Jace can only think of Clary. Clary herself freezes. And Simon the Mundane, who's been told to wait in the car, saves the day with his archery*

training from camp.
(Frankel)

Agramon

Agramon, the Demon of Fear, transforms into a person's greatest fear and scares him or her to death. "When it is done feeding on your terror, it kills you, presuming you are still alive at that point" (*City of Ashes* 256). He can escape his summoning pentagram when the summoner fears his escape, in a twisted loophole. When "formless" he is a black cloud with glowing eyes, enormous, with eyes the size of saucers. "Of course, he is a metaphor for facing fear as the teens must do: Maia sees her abusive brother, Jace confronts both his love for Clary and his fear of his father, and beats the second with the help of a Fearless rune. This gives him the power to confront the other and promise to only be Clary's brother" (Frankel). Clare adds:

> *It would make sense if Agramon were among the less-resistant-to-nonruned weapons. He doesn't need that resistance. He literally terrifies his prey to death, becoming the manifestation of their greatest fears. Even the toughest warriors can barely raise a trembling pinky under his influence, let alone a sword. He has other defenses that make resistance to ordinary weapons seem trivial. A broken strut in the hands of Jace was able to destroy him (well, return him to his home dimension), but Jace was only able to get that close to*

him and still function because of the Fearless rune
Clary invented. (Was Jace's own angel blood a fac-
tor? Maybe. We have no way of knowing for cer-
tain.)
Agramon hates the Fearless rune, obviously.
(Clare Tumblr, July 2015)

Armaros

Armaros, according to his own report, was among the demons that fought Jonathan Shadowhunter. After, it spent a millennium trapped in a Pyxis kept in the London Institute, before it was freed and placed in an automaton. He announces, "For a billion years I rode the winds of the great abysses between the worlds. I fought Jonathan Shadowhunter on the plains of the Brocelind. For a thousand more years I lay trapped within the Pyxis. Now my master has freed me and I serve him" (*Clockwork Princess* 382). Of course, Tessa and her friends banish them all. Armaros means "accursed one." According to the Book of Enoch, he was the eleventh among the list of 20 leaders of a group of 200 fallen angels called "Watchers" – often associated with Nephilim.

Asmodeus

Asmodeus is one of the nine princes of Hell and father to Magnus Bane, the child he claims to be most proud of. Magnus memorably calls on him once to discover the truth about their relationship then never again until *City of Heavenly Fire*, as he knows all demonic bargains have a great cost. He is a child of Lilith and ruler of Edom. In Persia, Asmodeus was a chief of evil spirits, usually named as one of the seven princes of Hell with the dominion of lust. It is said he tempted Noah into drunkenness in the Bible story.

> *Asmodius is a great king, strong and mightie, he is seene with three heads, whereof the first is like a bull, the second like a man, the third like a ram, he hath a serpents taile, he belcheth flames out of his mouth, he hath feete like a goose, he sitteth on an infernall dragon, he carrieth a lance and a flag in his hand, he goeth before others, which are under the power of Amaymon. When the conjuror exerciseth this office, let him be abroad [brave], let him be warie [courageous] and standing on his feete; "if his cap be on his head" [if he is afraid he will be overwhelmed], he will cause all his dooings to be bewraied [divulged], which if he doo not, the exorcist shal be deceived by Amaymon in everie thing.*
> (*Pseudomonarchia Daemonum*)

When he appears in the book, he's tall and pale in a pure white suit, with cufflinks like flies. "His face was a human face, pale skin pulled tight over bone, cheekbones sharp as blades. He didn't have hair so much as a sparkling coronet of barbed wires" (*Heavenly Fire* 621). He also reveals that he destroys his warlock children to fuel his realm, so few remain.

In Jace and Clary's Wayland Manor basement visions, Lilith, the "Lady of Edom" predicts that the child will be more powerful than Asmodei (*City of Glass* 201). When the teens reach Edom, they discover the demons there are called asmodei, as they're children of Asmodeus. "Lilith reportedly wound up marrying Asmodeus (the demon of Wrath and Lust) around the thirteenth century; a number of tales from the Middle Ages show them as a couple" (Mack 200).

> *Asmodeus (Ashmedai in Hebrew, meaning "evil spirit") is the undisputed king of the demons of Hebrew lore. He has three heads that face different directions. One is the head of a bull, the second the head of a ram, and the third the head of an ogre. He has the legs and feet of a cock and he rides a fire-breathing lion. All of these animals are associated with lust, which is his specialty. His other power areas are wrath and revenge. He wreaks havoc in households and produces enmity between man and wife. His favorite place is the bedroom.*
> (Mack 187)

The Jewish Biblical Apocrypha and its Book of Tobit describes the young woman Sara, who was married to seven husbands, all of whom Asmodeus had killed. Another righteous man, her cousin Tobit, was struck blind.

> *And Raphael was sent to heal them both, that is, to scale away the whiteness of Tobit's eyes, and to give Sara the daughter of Raguel for a wife to Tobias the son of Tobit; and to bind Asmodeus the*

evil spirit; because she belonged to Tobias by right
of inheritance.
(Tobit 3:17)

All these stories cast him as a fearful adversary of temptation and lust, but one that can be fought off with courage and holiness.

Azazel

Upon summoning him, Magnus calls him a "Greater Demon, Lieutenant of Hell and Forger of Weapons" (*Lost Souls* 207). On being summoned, he taunts the group with slanted deals and takes their memories as payment. He wears a silver and gray pinstripe suit with elegant cuffs, with flaming eyes and teeth tipped in iron needles. He's still bound in eternal punishment to the jagged mountain of Duduael. A fallen angel, his name means "God Strengthens." Azazel once led the 200 angels called grigori who mated with mortal women. Thus, he taught women to incite lust and men other skills.

> *And Azazel taught the people (the art of) making*
> *swords and knives, and shields, and breastplates;*
> *and he showed to their chosen ones bracelets, dec-*
> *orations, (shadowing of the eye) with antimony,*
> *ornamentation, the beautifying of the eyelids, all*
> *kinds of precious stones, and all coloring tinctures*
> *and alchemy.*
> (Enoch 8:1)

Magnus quotes the Book of Enoch, describing Azazel: "And the whole earth has been corrupted by the works that were taught by Azazel. To him ascribe all sin." Chapter Eleven of *Lost Souls* is called, appropriately, "Ascribe All Sin"

After Azazel taught humanity forbidden knowledge, the angels Michael, Uriel, Raphael, and Gabriel petitioned God to end the human world. In response, God told Noah to build an ark, and then issued the following command:

> And again the Lord said to Raphael: "Bind Azâzêl hand and foot, and cast him into the darkness: and make an opening in the desert, which is in Dûdâêl, and cast him therein. And place upon him rough and jagged rocks, and cover him with darkness, and let him abide there for ever, and cover his face that he may not see light. And on the day of the great judgment he shall be cast into the fire. And heal the earth which the angels have corrupted, and proclaim the healing of the earth, that they may heal the plague, and that all the children of men may not perish through all the secret things that the Watchers have disclosed and have taught their sons. And the whole earth has been corrupted through the works that were taught by Azâzêl: to him ascribe all sin."
> (Enoch 9:4-8)

Baal

Baal was a Moabite god, with a name meaning "Lord." As a competitor with the religion of the Bible, he soon became demonized. He's mentioned in the lore as a greater demon, of course.

Belial

BELIAL came last, than whom a Spirit more lewd
Fell not from Heaven, or more gross to love
Vice for it self: To him no Temple stood
Or Altar smoak'd; yet who more oft then hee
In Temples and at Altars, when the Priest
Turns Atheist, as did ELY'S Sons, who fill'd
With lust and violence the house of God.
In Courts and Palaces he also Reigns
And in luxurious Cities, where the noyse
Of riot ascends above thir loftiest Towrs,
And injury and outrage: And when Night
Darkens the Streets, then wander forth the Sons
Of BELIAL, flown with insolence and wine.
(Milton, Book I)

From the Hebrew "Bliol," meaning "Wicked One," Belial is the demon of lies. Some call him the father of Lucifer and the first demon expelled from Heaven. One of the Dead Sea scrolls, The War of the Sons of Light Against the Sons of Darkness, describes Belial leading the Sons of Darkness. He and his demons are a source of hostility and corruption in the world: "But for corruption thou hast made Belial, an angel of hostility. All his dominions are in darkness, and his purpose is to bring about wickedness and guilt. All the spirits that are associated with him are but angels of destruction."

> Some saie that the king Beliall was created imme-
> diatlie after Lucifer, and therefore they thinke that
> he was father and seducer of them which fell being
> of the orders…He taketh the forme of a beautifull
> angell, sitting in a firie chariot; he speaketh faire,
> he distributeth preferments of senatorship, and the
> favour of friends, and excellent familiars: he hath
> rule over eightie legions, partlie of the order of
> vertues, partlie of angels; he is found in the forme
> of an exorcist in the bonds of spirits.
> (Pseudomonarchia Daemonum)

Belial demons attack Idris in *City of Glass*. They appear to be the army of Greater Demon Belial.

Hecate

Hecate is a Greek underworld goddess, mistress of whips, secrets, and dark places, guardian of crossroads. She is a death-crone, and as such, can offer much wisdom to seekers. However, as the patriarchy grew in ancient Greece, she became demonized. In medieval lore, Hecate is said to be responsible for the creation of vampires. The *Codex* explains:

> *The Greater Demon Hecate, sometimes (and con-*
> *fusingly) called "the Mother of Witches" was sum-*
> *moned in a massive blood-based sacrifice held in*
> *1444 A.D. at the Court of Wallachia in what is*
> *now Romania. The then-ruler of Wallachia, Vlad*
> *III, had a great circle of prisoners of war impaled*
> *on tall wooden spikes, and in exchange for this*
> *impressive sacrifice, Hecate transformed Vlad and*
> *the large majority of his court into the first vam-*
> *pires.*
> (90)

Hunger

Hunger is an obese, devil-like humanoid Greater Demon that devours everything he encounters. With a body is covered in hard, bony scales and a variety of chomping fanged mouths he is indeed the personification of need. This demon exists around the world, an all-encompassing force of greed and desperation.

Lilith

Lilith hails from Jewish legend surrounding the stories of the Bible. In these, she is Adam's first wife, created equal to him, before the biddable Eve.

> *After God created Adam, who was alone, He said,*
> *'It is not good for man to be alone' (Genesis 2:18).*
> *He then created a woman for Adam, from the*

earth, as He had created Adam himself, and called her Lilith. Adam and Lilith immediately began to fight. She said, 'I will not lie below,' and he said, 'I will not lie beneath you, but only on top. For you are fit only to be in the bottom position, while I am to be the superior one.' Lilith responded, 'We are equal to each other inasmuch as we were both created from the earth.' But they would not listen to one another. When Lilith saw this, she pronounced the Ineffable Name and flew away into the air. Adam stood in prayer before his Creator: 'Sovereign of the universe!' he said, 'the woman you gave me has run away.' At once, the Holy One, blessed be He, sent these three angels to bring her back.

"Said the Holy One to Adam, 'If she agrees to come back, fine. If not, she must permit one hundred of her children to die every day.' The angels left God and pursued Lilith, whom they overtook in the midst of the sea, in the mighty waters wherein the Egyptians were destined to drown. They told her God's word, but she did not wish to return. The angels said, 'We shall drown you in the sea.'

"'Leave me!' she said. 'I was created only to cause sickness to infants. If the infant is male, I have dominion over him for eight days after his birth, and if female, for twenty days.'

"When the angels heard Lilith's words, they
insisted she go back. But she swore to them by the
name of the living and eternal God: 'Whenever I
see you or your names or your forms in an
amulet, I will have no power over that infant.' She
also agreed to have one hundred of her children
die every day. Accordingly, every day one hundred
demons perish, and for the same reason, we write
the angels names on the amulets of young chil-
dren. When Lilith sees their names, she remem-
bers her oath, and the child recovers."
(Stern and Mirsky 183- 184)

This story appears in *The Alphabet of Ben Sirah*, a book of
Jewish magic and mysticism dating back to the first millennium. In fact, in older sources, she appears in the ancient
mythology of Samaria, Canaan, Babylonia, Persia, and Arabia.
Mesopotamian mythology mentions the Lilim, various she-
demons, and a Liltu bird perched in the goddess Inanna's garden.

Lilith is the most important Jewish femme fatale
of the succubus species (female demons who
engage in erotic activities with male humans while
they sleep) and the only spirit of her gender
referred to in the Bible. It is only a brief mention,
following a description of a wasteland inhabited
by jackals and hyenas: "And Lilith shall repose
there" (Isaiah 34:14). Ancient tributaries to the
powerful Lilith point to her major roles, all associ-

ated with night, with seduction in the form of a
temptress-succubus, and by the Middle Ages, also
with the death of human infants. Her biblical
mention may have been intended to refer to
ancient Babylonian demonesses called lilitu
(female night spirits) or to the Sumerian wind
demon Lil (wind). Also, the word "night" in
Hebrew is lilah, and the screech owl, lilit.
(Mack 198)

In the Targum Yerushalmi, the priestly blessing of Numbers 6:26 becomes: "The Lord bless thee in all thy doings, and preserve thee from the Lilim!" Thus in Jewish folklore, she is another goddess demonized by the new religion –she becomes a banished demon living in the deep caverns of the world, begetting monsters. Samael, angel of death, is her consort. She was thus an early succubus or even vampire to many people. Often she would appear at night to strangle newborn babies if she was not warded off. Protective wards and blessings came into fashion to repel her – it is just these protections that Jace needs to keep her from influencing him in dreams.

In the books she's half again the height of a human, naked, with gray skin fissured like lava. Her eyes are "writhing black snakes" (*Lost Souls* 470). She creates the Infernal Cup from her blood, just as she gave Valentine blood to create Sebastian.

In an ancient Aramaic charm used against Lilith,
a writ of divorce is served on her, and she is com-
manded to go forth stripped. The stripping of this
demoness somehow erases her power, as when one

strips an officer of his stripes or strips someone of their "dignity." Perhaps removing her illusory garb shows her for what she is ... For the nursery, the amulet inscribed with the names of angels, Senoy, Sansenoy, and Semangeloff has been used effectively for a long time.

(Mack 201)

The Lilith amulets often contained her name in the belief that "the deterrent element which frightens the Evil Spirit away are the mysterious names of the Evil Spirit" (Gaster 149). One amulet includes the following statement:

These are my names, Satrina, Lilith, Abito, Amizo, Izorpo, Kokos, Odam, Ita, Podo, Eilo, Patrota, Abeko, Kea, Kali, Batna, Talto, and Partash. Whoever knows these my names and writes them down causes me to run away from the newborn child.

(Gaster 149)

It is the sight of their names which "terrifies her away, and protects those who invoke their aid against the attacks of the child-stealing witch" (Gaster 150). Obviously, several of these are referenced in the series with the Church of Talto and its representative Satrina. While her many names serve her as a shield, another weapon against her were angel names. One Lilith incantation bowl contains the following inscription:

You are bound and sealed,
all you demons and devils and liliths,
by that hard and strong,
mighty and powerful bond with which are tied
Sison and Sisin....
The evil Lilith,
who causes the hearts of men to go astray
and appears in the dream of the night
and in the vision of the day,
Who burns and casts down with nightmare,
attacks and kills children,
boys and girls.
She is conquered and sealed
away from the house
and from the threshold of Bahram-Gushnasp son
of Ishtar-Nahid
by the talisman of Metatron,
the great prince
who is called the Great Healer of Mercy....
who vanquishes demons and devils,
black arts and mighty spells
and keeps them away from the house
and threshold of Bahram-Gushnasp, son of Ishtar-
Nahid.
Amen, Amen, Selah.
Vanquished are the black arts and mighty spells.
Vanquished the bewitching women,
they, their witchery and their spells,
their curses and their invocations,
and kept away from the four walls

*of the house of Bahram-Gushnasp, the son of
Ishtar-Hahid.
Vanquished and trampled down are the bewitch-
ing women –
vanquished on earth and vanquished in heaven.
Vanquished are their constellations and stars.
Bound are the works of their hands.
Amen, Amen, Selah.*
(qtd. in Patai 228f)

Alec adds that Warlocks are called Lilith's children "Because
she mothered demons and they in turn brought forth the race
of warlocks" (*Fallen Angels* 329).

Lucifer

Lucifer, like Morgenstern, is a name for the morning star,
Venus. This is a name of light, but given to a fallen angel who
defied God and abandoned heaven.

The Second Book of Enoch details the rebellion and fall of
Satan and a host of angels under his command. In *Paradise
Lost,* the rebellious angel is Lucifer (many readers consider the
two angels the same character, synonymous with the devil, but
not all accounts agree).

Marax

Marax is a Greater Demon whom Charlotte Branwell encountered when she was young. A barrister and his mundane

friends attempted to raise a demon, chanting and drawing pentagrams on the ground as a warlock might do for a summoning. He raised Marax, but the demon slaughtered him and his family when he didn't bind it correctly. Marax was never found. (*Clockwork Angel* 142-143). In demonology, he is a bull with the face of a man, an Earl and President of hell who commands thirty legions.

Marbas

Azazel calls Magnus the "Destroyer of the Demon Marbas" in *Lost Souls*. Trapped in a pyxis by Edmund Herondale, the demon Marbas takes a great revenge on his children before and during the events of *Clockwork Angel* and *Clockwork Prince*. When young Will Herondale released the demon after its twenty year imprisonment, the demon told him everyone who loved him would die. When his sister Ella died that night, Will fled and began a life of torment. Only when he encountered the demon at Benedict Lightwood's ball did he steal its tooth then summon it, with aid from Magnus Bane. When Magnus demanded Marbas lift the curse, the creature revealed it had all been a lie. Marbas is short with blue scales, reptilian features, scarlet eyes, a flat snakelike snout, and a long, yellowish barbed tail with a stinger. In the *Ars Goetia*, Marbas is a President of Hell and Master of the Seal, commanding 36 legions. He often appears as a lion when summoned and is skilled at locating lost treasures.

Moloch

Moloch is one of Hell's most fearsome demon warriors, with a form of smoke and oil. The Children of Israel knew Moloch as a foreign god who, like many local demons, demanded the sacrifice of babies. Thus they battled his followers, and worship of the demon was considered a horror. In *Paradise Lost*, Milton describes him as the first of Lucifer's fallen angels. He is a "horrid king besmeared with blood/Of human sacrifice, and parents' tears" (I.392-393) and "the fiercest Spirit/ That fought in Heav'n; now fiercer in despair" (II.44-45).

> *Somewhat confusingly, the name "Moloch" refers both to a Greater Demon known as one of the most fearsome demon warriors, a being of smoke and oil, and also to a species of lesser demons ("Molochs") that are minions and foot soldiers of the Greater Demon Moloch. Individuals of the species are man-size, dark, and made of thick roiling oil, with arms but only a formless liquid appendage instead of legs. Their primary weapon is the flames that stream from their empty eye sockets, and they are usually seen in large numbers rather than in isolation.*
> (*Codex* 72)

Jace and Luke fight these on Valentine's ship in *City of Ashes*.

Mrs. Dark

Mrs. Dark's sister Mrs. Black is a warlock. She, however, is a full eidolon demon, a shapechanger like Tessa. However, Tessa, unlike her, can read the minds of her personas. Further, Tessa can love. Mrs. Dark is tall and thin, her hair almost colorless. She, like her sister, wears bright clothes and gloves, used to hide their clawed hands with grey, thick skin "like an elephant's hide" with long talons (*Clockwork Angel* 45)—their demon marks. Both serve the Magister in the series and train Tessa in shapechanging. Her true form has "hard grey stone-like skin," yellow eyes, and a triple row of mouths with greenish fangs (*Clockwork Angel* 409).

Samael

The Kabbalah describes Samael as "the severity of God" or "the venom of God" and lists him as one of the archangels. When God needs to send his force to render judgment or punishment, it is Samael. In rabbinic literature, Samael is chief of the Satans and the angel of death. The Book of Enoch calls him the prince of demons and a magician. He is "that great serpent with 12 wings that draws after him, in his fall, the solar system" ("Revelation 12). The *Codex* links him with the serpent who tempted Adam and Eve (67). In most tales, he is a fallen angel, sometimes the angel of death, who becomes husband to Lilith after she leaves Adam. In the mystical book called *The Zohar*, Samael says: "...my entire domination is based on killing. And if I accept the Torah [Bible], there will no longer be wars. My rule is over the planet Maadim (Mars, the war planet) that indicates spilling of blood."

> *There was another angel in the seventh heaven, different in appearance from all the others, and of frightful mien. His height was so great, it would have taken five hundred years to cover a distance equal to it, and from the crown of his head to the soles of his feet he was studded with glaring eyes, at the sight of which the beholder fell prostrate in awe. "This one," said Metatron, addressing Moses, "is Samael, who takes the soul away from man." "Whither goes he now?" asked Moses, and Metatron replied, "To fetch the soul of Job the pious." Thereupon Moses prayed to God in these words, "O may it be Thy will, my God and the God of my fathers, not to let me fall into the hands of this angel."*
> (Ginsburg 308)

Stheno

The *Codex* names Stheno as the Greater Demon that killed Granville Fairchild, co-creator of the Accords and Charlotte Fairchild's father (250). With a name meaning "forceful," she was the oldest of the Greek Gorgons, Medusa and her sisters, known for snaky hair and a gaze that could turn people to stone. The daughter of titans Phorcys and Ceto, she and her middle sister Euryale were immortal and dwelt in the caverns beneath Mount Olympus.

Yanluo

Yanluo Wang, also called Yan Wang, is the demon who tortured Jem as a child and addicted him to the yin fen. In the Chinese underworld, he's the senior king of the ten courts, who looks into the former lives of the dead and assigns them to the appropriate court for punishments. His name may relate him to the great death god, Yama. In the underworld, men or women with merit are rewarded, while others are sentenced to worse lives or torture. In the Infernal Devices series, Will and Jem reflect a great deal on the great wheel of reincarnation and on whether their lives balance as good or evil. There's a clear connection in why Yanluo has sealed Jem's fate.

9

Demonarium

Abraxas

The letters of Abraxas add up to the number 365, the same count the Basilideans gave to the orders of spirits that emanated in succession from the Supreme Being. The word Abraxas (or Abrasax or Abracax) appears today engraved on ancient "Abraxas stones," often with a bird-headed, snake-tailed figure. They were used as protective amulets. Presumably Abraxis is a Greater Demon, with others so-named as his followers in the series.

Achaieral Demons

A group of them attack the London Institute in "Vampires, Scones, and Edmund Herondale," only to be fought off by a temporary alliance of Shadowhunters and Downworlders. Achaieral demons blot out the moon and the stars, engulfing the sky in total darkness. With sharp teeth, blade-like talons, and "wide wings scorched-black leather like the aprons of blacksmiths" they're formidable (138).

Amphisbaenas

Pliny the Elder in his *Natural History* describes a two-headed snake, with the second at the tail-end, both able to spit poison (35). This was a creature of Greek bestiaries. Isidore of Seville adds some centuries later: "The amphisbaena has two heads, one in the proper place and one in its tail. It can move in the direction of eaither head with a circular motion. Its eyes shine like lamps. Alone among snakes, the amphisbaena goes out in the cold" (4:20). "What to Buy the Shadowhunter Who Has Everything" describes them differently:

> *The amphisbaena demon had the wings and the*
> *trunk of a vast chicken. Mundane stories claimed*
> *that it had the head and tail of a snake, but that*
> *was in fact not true. Amphisbaena demons were*
> *covered in tentacles, with one very large tentacle*
> *containing an eye, and a mouth with snapping*
> *fangs.*
> (359)

Asuras

In India, the gods are the Suras and the demons the Asuras or "non-gods." Their story of fallen angels resembles that in the Bible. It is said, "the Devas gave up falsehood and adopted truth, while the Asuras gave up truth and adopted falsehood." The name is a general term for demons and giants: they symbolized evil, darkness, and drought. They and the gods were trapped in endless battles for supremacy (Mackenzie 63).

Behemoth and Leviathan

Behemoth and Leviathan are paired: one is the great monster of the land, the other, the waters.

> *And on that day were two monsters parted, a female monster named Leviathan, to dwell in the abysses of the ocean over the fountains of the waters. But the male is named Behemoth, who occupied with his breast a waste wilderness named Duidain, on the east of the garden where the elect and righteous dwell.*
> (Enoch 76:7-8)

A Jewish rabbinic legend describes a great battle which will take place between them at the end of time:

> *They will interlock with one another and engage in combat, with his horns the Behemoth will gore with strength, the fish [Leviathan] will leap to meet him with his fins, with power. Their Creator will approach them with his mighty sword [and slay them both]. Then, from the beautiful skin of the Leviathan, God will construct canopies to shelter the righteous, who will eat the meat of the Behemoth and the Leviathan amid great joy and merriment.*
> (*Artscroll* siddur, 719)

Behemoth demons, attacking Idris in *City of Glass* and New York in "The Rise of the Hotel DuMort," are said to "eat *everything.*" The one the heroes face resembles "a blind slug with teeth" and is difficult to kill because it's semi-corporeal (247). Clary meets another in *City of Heavenly Fire.*

Cecaelia

Magnus Bane is hired to summon one of these in "What to Buy the Shadowhunter Who Has Everything." A Cecaelia, or an octopus person, is a composite mythical being much like *The Little Mermaid*'s Ursula. With the head, arms and torso of a woman (more rarely a man) and below the torso, the tentacles of an octopus or squid as a form of mermaid or sea demon. They have origins in the Haida, Tligit, Tsimshian and Nootka tribes of North America. A Draugr in Norse mythology is occasionally represented as a seaweed-covered octopus person. Of course, the term "cecaelia" is of more modern origin, to replace the clunky "octopus person."

Croucher

One of these attacks Luke during the demon siege in *City of Glass*. The Croucher, a Mesopotamian demon of doorways and entrances, is one of the invisible *rabisu* ("the ones that lie in wait"). As the ancient texts tell, it's "a species that makes its presence so deeply felt that it instantly causes the hair of any mortal to stand on end." The texts warn, "Staying home will not prevent a run-in with a lurking rabisu like the Croucher, an embodiment of evil who lies invisibly in wait for its mortal victims at the threshold of each house" (Mack 183-184). Ancient mundanes used amulets, talismans, and incantations used against them.

Daevas

In ancient Persian mythology, daevas are disease-causing demons who battle every form of religion. Spirits of chaos and disorder, they are tiny, wicked genies in the holy book *The Younger Avesta*. They threaten the order of the world, human health, and the regularity of religious life.

Dahak Demons

Dahak demons in the series are poisonous – Clary fights some in *Lost Souls* and they nearly kill her. They are lizardlike with green brown skin and six tentaclelike legs. In Iranian mythology, Zahhāk is an evil figure, called Aži Dahāka in the texts of the *Avesta,* the earliest religious texts of Zoroastrianism. In the text, he is a three-headed monster, strong and cunning. He is the son of the god of evil, who battles the god of light. The name is related to "stinging snake." Thus he may be another greater demon, with these his followers.

Daimons

In ancient Greece, Hesiod refers to innumerable invisible daimons of two general types: the daimons of the hero cult (which the heroes of the

Golden Age became after death) that act as
guardian spirits, and the other daimons, evil spir-
its of disease that can cause harm.
(Mack XXXI)

While in many series, daimons are familiars, there is another, evil type mixed into ancient myth. Nonetheless, the first kind are more traditional. They are not particularly good or evil, and can be either, tying humans to fate and the larger cosmos. Plato explains famously in his Symposium: "The Daimon is an intermediary spirit, described as neither god nor mortal but something between them." (qtd. in Mack XXXI).

Dantalion

In demonology, Dantalion is a powerful Great Duke of Hell. He has thirty-six legions of demons under his command and lives in service to Baalzebul, Lord of the Seventh Hell. He is the 71st of 72 spirits in the *Lesser Key of Solomon:*

The Seventy-first Spirit is Dantalion. He is a Duke
Great and Mighty, appearing in the Form of a
Man with many Countenances, all Men's and
Women's Faces; and he hath a Book in his right
hand. His Office is to teach all Arts and Sciences
unto any; and to declare the Secret Counsel of any
one; for he knoweth the Thoughts of all Men and
Women, and can change them at his Will. He can
cause Love, and show the Similitude of any per-

son, and show the same by a Vision, let them be in what part of the World they Will. He governeth 36 Legions of Spirits; and this is his Seal, which wear thou, etc.

Catarina and Maia encounter one – presumably this demon lord's followers – in New York. "It was about the size of a large dog, but it resembled a ball of grayish, pulsing intestines, studded with malformed kidneys and nodes of pus and blood. A single yellow, weeping eye glared out from among the jumble of organs" (*Heavenly Fire* 504).

Dragonidae

The word is actually the taxonomical family name used to refer to dragons. These do in fact resemble dragons with scaly bodies and wings, explaining the origins of the myths on earth. The first seraph blade was used by an Iron Sister to battle a dragon (*Codex* 20-21). On earth, all cultures have dragons, which appear a cultural memory of terrifying lizards, beyond the prevalence of dinosaur bones.

> *The ancients conceived it as the embodiment of malignant and destructive power, and with attributes of the most terrible kind. Classic story makes us acquainted with many dreadful monsters of the dragon kind, to which reference will afterwards be more particularly made.*

It is often argued that the monsters of tradition are but the personification of solar influences, storms, the desert wind, the great deeps, rivers inundating their banks, or other violent phenomena of nature, and so, no doubt, they are, and have been; but the strange fact remains that the same draconic form with slight modifications constantly appears as the type of the thing most dreaded, and instead of melting into an abstraction and dying out of view, it has remained from age to age, in form, distinctly a ferocious flying reptile, until in the opinion of many the tradition has been justified by prosaic science. It is surprising to find that the popular conception of the dragon – founded on tradition, passed on through hundreds of generations – not only retains its identity, but bears a startling resemblance to the original antediluvian saurians, whose fossil remains now come to light through geological research, almost proving the marvellous power of tradition and the veracity of those who passed it on.

(Vinycomb 59-60)

Though these demons are mostly extinct, Jace and Alec fight one at the start of *City of Ashes*.

Drevaks

These are spy or messenger demons in Clare's series, with several attacking Maia while watching Luke on Valentine's behalf. They resemble giant maggots "smooth, white, almost larval" (*City of Ashes* 218), though the spines in their mouths are poisonous. They smell like rotting garbage and roam in packs. Drevak demons apparently snore or make a related sound ("Pale Kings and Princes"). In *Clockwork Princess,* Benedict Lightwood turns into one, or something quite similar, thanks to demon pox. When Clary asks why the demons would attack Maia, Luke tells her: "Drevak demons aren't bloodsuckers and they definitely couldn't cause the kind of mayhem you saw in the Silent City. Mostly they're spies and messengers. I think Maia just got in its way" (*City of Ashes* 221). The name is Czech slang for clumsy, appropriate as they can't see.

Du'sien

Du'sien demons disguise themselves as police to chase down Clary in the first book. They are shapeshifters of course, and their true form is abstract and irregular, like a greenish-gray blob with a glowing black core. "Du sien" means "of one's own" in French, in a bit of a pun on "possession."

Eidolon

Eidolons are shapechanging demons like Mrs. Dark and Tessa's father in *The Infernal Devices.* Another appears in "The Whitechapel Fiend," and one is the first demon Clary sees at the Pandemonium Club. As the *Codex* adds, "Since there are dozens of these species, Shadowhunters typically use the term 'Eidolon' to refer to shape-shifting demons in general" (70). Mythologically, they are ghosts that possess the living. Several tales have been collected from Athens and India in the C1st A.D. concerning the prophet Apollonios of Tyana.

Philostratus in *Life of Apollonius of Tyana* from the first century describes several encounters with Eidolons (phantoms). A messenger brought forward a poor woman who described her sixteen-year-old son who had been for two years possessed by a Eidolon. She told the sages:

> *This child of mine is extremely good-looking, and*
> *therefore the Daimon is amorous of him and will*
> *not allow him to retain his reason, nor will he per-*
> *mit him to go to school, or to learn archery, nor*
> *even to remain at home, but drives him out into*
> *desert places and the boy does not even retain his*
> *own voice, but speaks in a deep hollow tone, as*
> *men do; and he looks at you with other eyes*
> *rather than with his own.*
> (3. 38 ff)

The ghost, itself restless after its wife's betrayal, insisted on keeping the boy with loud threats and bribes. The sages won the day by sending their own threats to the creature. In another encounter, this one in Athens:

> *The youth was, without knowing it, possessed by a*
> *Daimon; for he would laugh at things that no one*

*else laughed at, and then he would fall to weeping
for no reason at all, and he would talk and sing to
himself. Now most people thought that it was the
boisterous humour of the youth which led him
into such excesses; but he was really the mouth-
piece of a Daimon, though it only seemed a
drunken folic in which on that occasion he was
indulging. Now when Apollonios gazed on him,
the Eidolon (Ghost) in him began to utter cries of
fear and rage, such as one hears from people who
are being branded or wracked; and the Eidolon
(Ghost) swore that he would leave the young man
alone and never take possession of any man again.*
(4.20 ff)

Elapid Demons

Scientifically, this is the name for the cobra family. Of course, these take the form of enormous poisonous cobra-headed creatures. Their bodies are jointed and insectile, with a dozen skittering legs that end in jagged claws. In Prague, during *City of Lost Souls*, a swarm of Elapids attack Sebastian, Clary, and Jace, though the Shadowhunters win the battle.

Eluthied

Jonathan Morgenstern hunts an Eluthied demon, and then takes over his partner Sebastian Verlac's identity. The demon is a shapechanger, disguised as a dark-haired girl (described in "A Dark Transformation," a short story in the special edition of *City of Lost Souls*).

Facemelter

This one is mentioned, with little detail, in the Codex. It says simply "Self-explanatory" (70). Apparently it is.

Foraii Demon

Marax or Morax, a human-faced bull, is an Earl of Hell and controller of thirty legions. "Morax, alias Foraii, a great earle and a president, he is seene like a bull, and if he take unto him a man's face, he maketh men wonderfull cunning in astronomie, & in all the liberall sciences" (*Pseudomonarchia Daemonum*). Will buys Foraii demon powders at the beginning of *Clockwork Prince*.

Gorgons

These monsters, briefly mentioned in the *Codex* (64), are snake-haired monsters like Medusa, whose gaze turns victims to stone. They hail from Greek myth.

Hellhounds

Lilith commands hellhounds with shimmering red eyes and spiked mace-like tails in *City of Fallen Angels*. These black canines vaguely resemble Doberman Pinschers, but larger.

Their presence in myth dates back to Greek guardian dog of hell Cerberus. Dogs were said to be sacred to underworld goddess Hecate, adding to the lore.

Husa Demons

Clary tangles with "a gaggle of Husa demons" in *City of Heavenly Fire* (685). This name does not appear in bestiaries, suggesting it's Clare's invention.

Hydra

This Greek monster was defeated by Hercules in one of his labors. It famously resided near water, giving it its name. These are traditionally treasure guardians with at least three snake heads, sometimes hundreds. The ones in Clare's lore are blind, finding prey through sound and smell. One guards the Church of Talto.

Iblis

Iblis demons attack Magnus Bane in Idris, leaving Alec to rescue him in *City of Glass.* According to Muslim belief, the djinn are powerful beings who possess free will, unlike angels, who do not. They were created from a smokeless fire, while angels are made of light.

When God created Adam, he commanded all the angels and Iblis the djinn to prostrate to Adam, who was formed in God's image. Iblis refused to obey, and thus rebelled against

God. For this God cast him out of the Garden, and intended to punish him. Iblis begged God to delay the punishment until the Last Day (the Day of Judgment): this God granted. Many equate him with Satan. Thus iblis, like djinn, are formed of black smoke with burning eyes.

Imp

"The common Imp is a small humanoid with the characteristics of a typical Western devil—horns, forked tail, et cetera. They are not very dangerous individually but can become a problem when encountered in swarms of more than two hundred, as is occasionally reported" (*Codex* 71-72). In the New York Institute library is a book titled *The Care and Feeding of Your Pet Imp* in *Lost Souls.* The original imps were messenger spirits from Germanic folklore, more mischievous than evil. Eventually they became twined with the concept of familiars and witches' helpers (Bane).

Kappa

Kappa, only mentioned in the *Codex*, are Japanese water demons. With a protective shell and sharp beak, they leap out of water to drag mundanes to their deaths.

Kuri

In *City of Ashes,* Valentine summons these spider demons to his boat. They have eight pincer-tipped arms and poisoned fangs. According to the Hausa people of West Africa, Kuri is the demon of paralysis, in this case, a black hyena spirit (Bane).

Malphas Demon

Malphas was the President of Deceivers and commands forty legions of demons. Often appearing as a large black bird, he has great talent at building towers and strongholds when summoned. Gabriel Lightwood would rather be "dropped into a vat of Malphas venom" than apologize to Will in *Clockwork Angel.*

Memory Demon (show only)

A demon that can eat someone's memories and keep them safe. It's willing to return Clary's in exchange for more memories, but Alec is shaken (ep 4) and lets the demon loose. Clary manages to slay it. Azazel takes this plot in the books.

Oni

Japanese Oni demons ingest entire vineyards of wine in one sitting and spit out rivers when they laugh. They have flat faces with mouths that run ear to ear and a third eye. Winged and horned as well, they have three taloned toes on each foot and three clawed fingers on each hand. "Excessive in their behavior, all Oni drink and eat too much, randomly abduct young women, and are revoltingly uncouth. These demons are always present when disaster strikes, and are also associated with disease. They bear the souls of the wicked to the underworld" (Mack 116). Valentine summons Oni to his ship in *City of Ashes* and they attack Idris in *City of Glass.*

> *Despite their great powers, they are so preoccupied with satisfying excessive bodily needs that their intelligence is diminished. They remain vulnerable to human trickery and ingenuity. Shocking an Oni is a good way out of a bad situation. They can also be given tasks, such as counting holes in a sieve, that keep them distracted and occupied while the victim escapes. Throwing dry peas about in four directions, done at the Oni-yarahi ceremony, chases the Oni away.*
> (Mack 117-118)

Rahab Demon

In Clare's world, these are blind lizard men with poisonous stingers on their tongues and powerful whiplike tails. In Jewish folklore and a few Biblical references, Rahab is the name of a sea-demon, the water-dragon of darkness and chaos, who shakes the waters to produce the waves.

Rakshasas

The Rakshasas are the enemies of man. These demons are "night prowlers"; they have greatest power after "the first forty seconds of grey twilight preceding nightfall." Shapechangers, they appear as tigers, bears, or great monkeys in various colors.

In the Ramayana they are found associated with the Asuras of Ceylon; a spy enters a demon dwelling and sees them in all their shapes, some frightfully deformed, with small bodies and long arms; some as grotesque dwarfs, others as horrible giants with long projecting teeth; some with one eye, others with three eyes; some with one leg, two legs, or three, or even four; and some with heads of serpents, horses, or elephants. In the Mahabharata the Rakshasas are like gorillas; they have arrow-shaped ears, big red eyes, and red hair and beards, and mouths like caves; they feast on human beings and cattle.
(Mackenzie 67)

Raum

Raum demons with slick, gray-white tentacles tipped with red suckers, crown the suckers with a cluster of tiny, poisonous needle-like teeth. They are the size of an elongated human with "dead white, scaled skin, a black hole for a mouth, bulging toad-like eyes" (*City of Ashes* 236). Though speechless, they can make a hooting noise and are clever. They are generally sent on missions of retrieval – Valentine sends them to kidnap Maia Roberts.

In the great demon hierarchy, Raum is a Great Earl who commands thirty legions.

Raum, or Raim is a great earle, he is seene as a
crowe, but when he putteth on humane shape, at
the commandement of the exorcist, he stealeth
woonderfullie out of the kings house, and carrieth
it whether he is assigned, he destroieth cities, and
hath great despite unto dignities, he knoweth
things present, past, and to come, and reconcileth
freends and foes, he was of the order of thrones,
and governeth thirtie legions.
(Pseudomonarchia Daemonum)

Raveners

"Raveners are search-and-destroy machines," Alec explains in
City of Bones. "They act under orders from warlocks or powerful demon lords." Raveners with alligator heads are the first
demons Clary meets (aside from the boy at the Pandemonium
Club) as they attack Clary's apartment. One speaks to her,
planning to eat her, and she kills it with a Sensor. These appear
invented by Clare, rather than adapted from Demonologies.

It was crouched against the floor, a long, scaled
creature with a cluster of flat black eyes set dead
center in the front of its domed skull. Something
like a cross between an alligator and a centipede,
it had a thick, flat snout and a barbed tail that
whipped menacingly from side to side. Multiple
legs bunched underneath it as it readied itself to
spring.
(City of Bones)

Scorpios

This type of demon resembles a scorpion with its long, barbed, needle-tipped tail. It has a wrinkled face, the agile hands "of a huge monkey," rolling, yellow eyes, and teeth like broken needles. Hissing, it stings victims with its tail using cobra speed. Inquisitor Herondale dies defending Jace from one of these in *City of Ashes*. They appear invented by Clare, though giant scorpions are common in desert mythology.

Shadow

"A personal Shadow rests in the depths of the unconscious of every person, ready and waiting to spring." The Shadow includes all those aspects of a person's nature that he believes unacceptable. Carl Jung describes it as a person's darker dimension or inner demon – the part one hides from others and even from oneself. "The Shadow lies at the threshold of the unexpressed self, at the border between the known and the unknown" (Mack 265). Shadowy figures in hooded robes are popular as monsters throughout world folklore, appearing in many fantasy series. The ancients of earth believed a man's shadow could detach and go wandering, but "a living person's loss of shadow, however, was equated with the loss of the soul" (Walker 353).

Shax

These are brood parasites that lay eggs in people's bodies and have strong senses of smell (*Clockwork Angel* 4-5). A Shax demon is sent by the Dark Sisters to track a runaway girl, then killed by Will Herondale. He later mentions that misericord blades are the best to pierce their armored carapaces. As an adult, Will is bitten by a Shax demon and nearly dies. Jem sits with him all night to ensure his recovery.

Shax is "a darke and a great marquesse, like unto a storke, with a hoarse and subtill voice" (*Pseudomonarchia Daemonum*). The Forty-fourth Spirit, he is a Great Marquis of Hell with thirty legions of demons under his command. Shax is depicted as a stork that speaks with a hoarse but subtle voice; his voice changes into a beautiful one once he enters the magic triangle of his summoner.

Skeletons

A demon that looks like animated skeleton wrapped in Tibetan prayer flags attacks in *City of Ashes,* a katana in its demonic hand. Another carrying a bloodied hatchet attacks in *City of Glass.* Simon considers it "like the image of Death from a medieval woodcut (*City of Glass* 468).

Vermis Demon

Isabelle fights one in *Fallen Angels* and dispatches it with her stiletto heel. In fact, the name is Latin for worm, as is the appearance.

Vermithrall

Vermithrall, mentioned in the *Codex*, is a worm demon that collects into writhing colonies and form a humanoid-shaped, lumbering monstrous mass (74).

Vetis demons

Sebastian, Jace, and Clary meet with one named Mirek in Prague. "Tall and human-shaped with gray skin and ruby-red eyes, a mouth full of pointed teeth that jutted every which way, and long, serpentine arms that ended in heads like an eel's – narrow, evil-looking, and toothy" (*Lost Souls* 284). "Nothing but Shadows" introduces a Vetis demon with a red-eyed, sharp-toothed face, "its shape almost human but not quite, dragging its gray, scaly body through the fallen leaves. James [Herondale] saw the eel-like heads on its arms lifting, like the heads of pointer dogs out hunting." Apparently they hoard sparkly things.

10

Other Creatures

Ghosts

"Not all Shadowhunters could hear ghosts, unless the ghosts chose to be heard, but Will was one of those who could (*Clockwork Prince* 1). He enters a graveyard and negotiates with the ghost Old Molly, buying demon powders from her. She's only interested in one type of payment – rings that might be her old wedding ring, "that lost piece of her past that would finally allow her to die, the anchor that kept her trapped in the world" (*Clockwork Prince* 4).

Jessamine becomes a ghost herself, guarding the institute she once betrayed. In the short stories, she's seen protecting the children of the London Institute, then defending it against Sebastian in *City of Heavenly Fire*. After Simon's ascension in the *Shadowhunter Academy* short stories, she carries another Lovelace away and, it's implied, finally earns some peace.

The *Codex* notes that some Shadowhunters (like a few Mundanes) have the sight and can detect ghosts, but Marks can't enhance this skill. Ghosts have hollow, empty eyes and leech heat from their surroundings (*Codex* 131-132). These spirits parallel the popular view of ghosts, and in particular a Jewish one:

The spirits of the dead were believed to remain in close contact with the living, retaining their old interests, and often performing signal service for their relatives and friends who still inhabited this earth in the flesh. Provocation, it is true, might stir them up to strike back at their enemies. But in general the dead were not regarded as malevolent; rather were they seen as wistful, harmless shades haunting the graves which shelter their bones.
(Trachtenberg 31)

Zombies

Clary shook her head. "Don't stop there. I suppose there are also, what, vampires and werewolves and zombies?"

"Of course there are," Jace informed her. "Although you mostly find zombies farther south, where the voudun priests are."

"What about mummies? Do they only hang around Egypt?"

"Don't be ridiculous. No one believes in mummies."
(*City of Bones*)

According to Vodou, the soul consists of two aspects: the *gros bon ange* (big good angel) and the *ti bon ange* (little good angel). The first controls biological functions, and the second, personality and individual identity. Since folklore suggests these can being separated, the lore of the zombie is created. In Haitian Vodou, zombies were corpses raised by a *bokor* (sorcerer) to be his slaves, as they lacked free will.

11

Downworlders

The Angel Raziel himself says that warlocks, fairies, werewolves and even vampires all have souls, unlike demons (*City of Glass* 493). Nonetheless, many Shadowhunters treat Downworlders, as they call them, with total disdain. Clary calls them out on this prejudice, asking, "So they're good enough to let live, good enough to make your food for you, good enough to flirt with — but not really good enough? I mean, not as good as people."

Hodge notes that these prejudices are still prominent in some of the older Shadowhunter families, because "it is easier to confront a threat as a mass, a group, not individuals who must be evaluated one by one" (*City of Bones*). The tradition of spoils, in which Shadowhunters can steal the Downworlders' property after killing them, emphasizes how there is a particularly selfish component to the ancient prejudices. Medieval witch trials had a similar system, motivating biased trials and cruelty.

Becoming a werewolf or vampire is often believed to be a demon disease, transmitted to humans through a bite or scratch (*Clockwork Angel* 174). It's said that the two demon species are at war with each other, leading to an automatic animosity between the two species. Likewise, the fairies and warlocks dislike Shadowhunters but also each other. "The Fair

Folk looked down upon warlocks for their willingness to perform magic for money. Meanwhile the warlocks scorned the Fair Folk for their inability to lie, their hidebound customs, and their penchant for pettily annoying mundanes by curdling their milk and stealing their cows" (*Heavenly Fire* 257).

The Accords were finalized ten years before the writing of the Codex, with their origins explored in "Vampires, Scones and Edmund Herondale." In this story of 1857, the Shadowhunters make laws for the Downworlders, and young fanatic Ralf Scott demands that the Shadowhunters agree to only kill Downworlders who have broken the laws. "We will want guarantees that no Downworlders whose hands are clean of Mundane blood will be slaughtered. We want a law that states that any Shadowhunter who does strike down an innocent Downworlder will be punished," he insists (130). They were finally signed in 1872 and again every fifteen years ("Lady Midnight Excerpt").

On one of these occasions, Valentine plans to destroy the Downworld representatives with his Circle. He fails, thanks to Jocelyn and Luke. "When the Downworlders saw the Clave turn on Valentine and his Circle in their defense, they realized Shadowhunters were not their enemies. Ironically, with his insurrection Valentine made the Accords possible," Hodge says (*City of Bones*). Through the series, Downworlders gain more power and respect, from the days when Shadowhunters collected spoils and threw away the plates their Downworld guests used to 2007's *City of Glass*, where they earn four Council seats.

Of course, many of the memorable Downworld leaders are lost in the Dark War that follows. After the war, the Shadowhunter Academy is reopened to encourage Ascendant hopefuls to come fill their depleted ranks. Also the Scholomance is reestablished. Julian adds, "It existed before the first Accords were signed, and when the Council was betrayed by faeries, they insisted on opening it again. The Scholomance does research, trains Centurions ..." ("Lady Midnight Excerpt"). These Centurions are special warriors who deal with the Fair Folk. "Born to Endless Night" describes the shifting balance of power among Downworlders after the Dark War:

> *Old structures that had held their society in place*
> *for centuries, like the Praetor Lupus, had been*
> *destroyed in the war. The faeries were waiting to*
> *revolt. And the werewolf and vampire clans of*
> *New York both had brand-new leaders. Both Lily*
> *and Maia were young to be leaders, and had suc-*
> *ceeded entirely unexpectedly to leadership. Both of*
> *them had found themselves, due to inexperience*
> *and not lack of trying, in trouble.*

Maia and Lily find themselves meeting at Magnus and Alec's house, drawing on the knowledge of all the Shadowhunters as well as Magnus's experience. They have an informal council dealing with Downworlder discipline within their community. Thus the group form their own council, and word spreads that in New York, the Downworlders and Shadowhunters have a special informal meeting place.

Wild Hunt

*The Cwˆn Annwn are the hounds of the under-
world, said to hunt on the mountainside of Cadair
Idris [in Clockwork Princess]. Linked to the legend
of the Wild Hunt (which is mentioned in City of
Lost Souls), the Welsh version of this tale, which
extends across other cultures in the area, the
Cwˆn are associated with the migration of geese,
and supposedly hunt only on certain days.*
(Spencer, Kindle Locations 3262-3265)

The Wild Hunt serves its own laws and harvests the dead after
a battle. Jace calls them "Gabriel's hounds" and "The Wild
Host" – fairies that refuse service in both Fairie courts. "They
ride across the sky, pursuing an eternal hunt. On one night a
year, a mortal can join them—but once you've joined the hunt
you can never leave it" (*Lost Souls* 230).

12

Witches and Warlocks

Jace tells Clary, "Human beings are not magic users. It's part of what makes them human. Witches and warlocks can only use magic because they have demon blood" (*City of Bones*). Clare's witches and warlocks are human-demon crossbreeds, and thus sterile. Jace explains that they are the strongest of the Downworlders, since they're the direct offspring of demons (*City of Bones*). Cthonian, the warlock language, means "of the Earth" in Greek, relating to underworld deities of darkness, chaos, and evil.

In Clare's series, Greenpoint in New York is warlock territory. They're immortal, though they're also sterile like mules. They call themselves "Lilith's children," as they do get their powers from demons. However, like werewolves and vampires, their transformation is not of their choice – the demons sleep with their mothers and thus create the children, who are often shunned. In ancient myth, incubi and succubi were these seducer demons, who interfered with sleeping people to produce demonic children.

The word comes from *waerloga*, "deceiver," referencing one who has made a pact with the devil for his powers. Also the classic term for a male witch. Historically, the superstitious believed witches gained their powers thus and in return received a "devil's mark" – any kind of abnormal birthmark.

These are reflected in the "warlocks' marks" of this series like Magnus's cat eyes or other characters' blue or green skin. The books list bat wings, goats' feet, and antlers, among other traits (*City of Glass* 412). Nonetheless, warlocks bleed red like humans.

The related species ifrits have marks as well (in the books, talons and red or orange skins) – they're "warlocks without powers." Some run a demon drug den in London (*Clockwork Prince* 191). Clancy, doorman at Taki's, is one. In Middle Eastern folklore, these are a class of infernal djinn dwelling in isolated ruins, though often in complex social structures. They are invulnerable to weapons but susceptible to magic.

13

Vampires

"We want you to tell us about vampires."

Simon grinned. "What do you want to know? Scariest is Eli in Let the Right One In, cheesiest is late-era Lestat, most underrated is David Bowie in The Hunger. Sexiest is definitely Drusilla, though if you ask a girl, she'll probably say Damon Salvatore or Edward Cullen. But . . ." He shrugged. "You know girls."

Julie's and Beatriz's eyes were wide. "I didn't think you'd know so many!" Beatriz exclaimed. "Are they … are they your friends?"

"Oh, sure, Count Dracula and I are like this," Simon said, crossing his fingers to demonstrate. *"Also Count Chocula. Oh, and my BFF Count Blintzula. He's a real charmer …" He trailed off as he realized no one else was laughing. In fact, no one seemed to realize he was joking. "They're from TV," he prompted them. "Or, uh, cereal."*
("The Lost Herondale")

Despite Simon's pop culture jokes, there are many vampires in the Shadowhunters' world and indeed the old stories are true. In Clare's world, vampires were created in 1444 A.D. in modern day Romania – in a public ceremony, Vlad III impaled many prisoners and beseeched Hecate to transform him and his court (*Codex* 90). More vampires are created when humans taste a vampire's blood and are bitten in turn, drained to the point of death.

In the series, vampires cannot enter hallowed ground. Further, vampires have a complex and obscure sense of etiquette and will kill those among them who break it (*Clockwork Angel* 223). Clannish as they are, they believe killing one of their own is the worst possible crime. Vampires forbid their people from having relationships with werewolves as the two species are natural enemies (*Clockwork Angel* 192). They can't say the name of God, ordinarily – Camille tells Simon she can say it because she no longer believes, unlike him.

Isabelle notes that legends of vampires repelled by garlic or compelled to count spilled grains of rice aren't true (*Fallen Angels* 7). Likewise, vampires can see themselves in mirrors, though Simon considers that vampires might wish they couldn't see themselves as they no longer recognize themselves in the reflections (*Fallen Angels* 119). They do have the power of fascination, mesmerizing people with just their voices. They're sensitive to their own grave dirt and vulnerable to many holy symbols, like blessed metal, holy water, and symbols of their own religion.

As all other demoniacal monsters the Vampire
fears and shrinks from holy things. Holy Water

burns him as some biting acid; he flies from the
sign of the Cross, from the Crucifix, from Relics,
and above all from the Host, the Body of God. All
these, and other hallowed objects render him pow-
erless. He is conquered by the fragrance of
incense. Certain trees and herbs are hateful to
him, the whitethorn (or buckthorn) as we have
seen, and particularly garlic. (Summers 131)

The word vampyr likely derives from the Mediterranean vam-pir, "blood-monster" or from Russia from the words for blood-drunkenness. When Simon is first transformed, his thirst is blood-drunkenness, indeed, as a truly uncontrollable need. Almost every culture has a myth about the angry dead, risen from the grave to suck the blood of the living. The monsters are the Adze in West Africa, Jiāngshī in China, Sigbin in the Philippines, the Cihuateteo to the Aztecs, and Draugr to the Vikings. The Celtic Leanan Sidhe drains the life from her victims like a succubus (Curran 23-30).

John Heinrich Zopfius in his Dissertatio de Uam-
piris Seruiensibus, Halle, 1733, says: "Vampires
issue forth from their graves in the night, attack
people sleeping quietly in their beds, suck out all
their blood from their bodies and destroy them.
They beset men, women and children alike, spar-
ing neither age nor sex. Those who are under the
fatal malignity of their influence complain of suf-
focation and a total deficiency of spirits, after
which they soon expire. Some who, when at the

> *point of death, have been asked if they can tell*
> *what is causing their decease, reply that such and*
> *such persons, lately dead, have arisen from the*
> *tomb to torment and torture them."*
> (Summers 1-2)

Vampires are considered the unblessed or vengeful dead, and that is the reason holy symbols repel them. They essentially prey on the living and take their souls to sustain themselves.

> *In some Slavonic countries it is thought that a*
> *Vampire, if prowling out of his tomb at night may*
> *be shot and killed with a silver bullet that has*
> *been blessed by a priest. But care must be taken*
> *that his body is not laid in the rays of the moon,*
> *especially if the moon be at her full, for in this case*
> *he will revive with redoubled vigour and malevo-*
> *lence.*
> (Summers 208-209)

The Bible forbids drinking blood, the essence of life, which is often equated with the soul. Symbolically, the people of the Bible may consume the animal's body but not its spirit. In the original Hebrew, this word is often translated as soul. It is written:

> *If any man whosoever of the house of Israel, and*
> *of the strangers that sojourn among them, eat*
> *blood I will set my face against his soul, and will*

cut him off from among his people: Because the life of the flesh is in the blood: and I have given it to you, that you may make atonement with it upon the altar for your souls, and the blood may be for an expiation for the soul...Since then the very essence of life, and even more, the spirit or the soul in some mysterious way lies in the blood we have a complete explanation why the vampire should seek to vitalize and rejuvenate his own dead body by draining the blood from the veins of his victims.

(Summers 14-15)

Human subjugates, or darklings, swear themselves to a vampire's service in Clare's work. They drink that vampire's blood, binding themselves to the longer-lived being. The vampire blood makes the darklings "stronger and healthier, and makes them live longer. That's why it's not against the Law for a vampire to feed on a human" (*Fallen Angels* 9). When they die, the blood makes them into vampires. Subjugates stare at their masters with blind adoration and look forward to the day when they will be turned. At parties, they willingly open veins for their masters and any friends the master wishes (*Clockwork Angel* 236). They live on vampire and animal blood, which keeps them in a state of suspended animation where they age quite slowly (*Fallen Angels* 10). The Accords of the twenty-first century forbid the creation of Darklings, though ones previously made are permitted.

14

Werewolves

Werewolves hail from Western Europe, though there are older mentions in world folklore. Romans, Celts, and Norse each had their versions, as did the Native Americans. In the French and Germanic traditions, lycanthropy, making oneself into a were creature through a special belt or magical ointments, was seen as witchcraft, and thus, as a sin against God. "Pointed ears, hair on palms, large claws, paws, eyebrows that are connected over the bridge of the nose, or hair between the shoulder blades are common werewolf features" (Mack 235). The *Loup Garou* is a French bayou werewolf species – the name may come from "Loup, gardez-vous," which means "Wolf, watch out!" (Mack 239). The legend migrated to Louisiana, where the creature became a *rougarou,* a human who wore a wolf's head for 101 days.

Clare's series has lone heroes killing the pack leader to take his place – Luke abandons his pack in the forests outside Idris, but claims one near Columbus Park. Some werewolves are born to werewolf parents and others are bitten, with a large chance of contracting the demon disease. "For those of us who are turned by a bite, those first few years are key. The demon strain that causes lycanthropy causes a whole raft of other changes—waves of uncontrollable aggression, inability to control rage, suicidal anger and despair" Jordan Kyle explains (*Fallen Angels* 142).

Jordan appears in the second trilogy to introduce Praetor Lupus, the "Wolf Guardians." They monitor Downworlders and help them adjust, especially after a sudden transformation. In the time of *The Infernal Devices*, the group was founded by Woolsey Scott, who was determined to have protection for his people when the Shadowhunters wouldn't give them Council seats in the nineteenth century.

In myth, a silver bullet is the only sure way to kill a werewolf, though other methods have been recorded:

> *A pitchfork can be used to strike a vulnerable spot*
> *between the eyebrows and allow time for escape,*
> *and special gray stones are said to keep the species*
> *at a distance. Voluntary Werewolves are able to*
> *become human again when a special formula is*
> *uttered. However, if the human who knows the*
> *formula dies, the Werewolf is doomed to remain*
> *one.*
> (Mack 238)

Silver, a metal of purity, was used around the world to repel the unholy. The first recorded instance of silver being used to combat werewolves is from a werewolf epidemic in the city of Greifswald in 1640. As werewolves were battling the humans and beginning to outnumber them, a group of students thought of melting silver down for musketballs. The town was saved (Konstantinos 79). In the 1760s, Jean Chastel slew the famous Beast of Gévaudan with silver bullets that had been made from a chalice blessed by a priest (Konstantinos 79). Other recorded cures include hitting the wolf three times on the head hard enough to draw blood, or reminding it of its human nature by calling it by name (Konstantinos 89-91).

In films and modern novels, werewolves are generally created by another werewolf's bite. This theme appears in *Harry Potter, Buffy,* and many other series.

> *The concepts that a werewolf bite could transform a person into a werewolf, and that the change would occur on the following full moon are barely seen in folklore and instead originate in the popular 1941 movie, Wolf Man. This film also introduced the use of silver to repel the beasts and the half-wolf, half-man form seen in some popularized werewolves. Wolf Man was a commercial success, and many other werewolf films followed, including I Was a Teenage Werewolf, American Werewolf in London, and The Howling. These perpetuated the concepts introduced in Wolf Man and made concepts like the full moon and silver bullets a permanent part of the trope.*
> (Frankel)

Folkloric accounts varied more. Some people were born to werewolf parents, or were born with the curse because of the circumstances of their birth. Being born on Christmas Day, the full moon, or another time of near-magical light in deep darkness could do it. So could being a man's seventh illegitimate son, called a *bitang* in Romanian folklore (Konstantinos 37). A similar tradition exists in Argentina and Brazil. In the Balkans, eating a certain plant could begin the transformation. Many people blamed drinking from a wolf's pawprint or eating meat a wolf had killed. Others deliberately made themselves into werewolves with spells and incantations. One famous ritual called for a girdle of wolf skin and a magical salve.

Recorded werewolf tales generally followed one of a few patterns: children would disappear from a town and the murderer would claim he'd been killing children, and possibly eating them, when he transformed into a wolf. He would be executed by the court of law without ever demonstrably transforming. Being a werewolf was linked with witchcraft and the devil: From 1520 to 1630 in France, there were 30,000 court cases dealing with werewolves and witchcraft (Konstantinos 49). Other legends would see a husband or wife noting the spouse's disappearance at certain times. He or she would encounter a wolf, perhaps even be attacked by it, and shoot it or cut off a paw. The next day, the spouse would have the exact same injury. Here are a few of the court cases:

Pierre Bourgot gave a full confession at his trial of his shapeshifting with Michel Verdung:

> In a wood near Chastel Charnon we met with
> many others whom I did not recognize; we
> danced, and each had in his or her hand a green
> taper with a blue flame. Still under the delusion
> that I should obtain money, Michel persuaded me
> to move with the greatest celerity, and in order to
> do this, after I had stripped myself, he smeared me

with a salve, and I believed myself then to be transformed into a wolf. I was at first somewhat horrified at my four wolf's feet, and the fur with which I was covered all at once, but I found that I could now travel with the speed of the wind. This could not have taken place without the help of our powerful master, who was present during our excursion, though I did not perceive him till I had recovered my human form. Michel did the same as myself.

When we had been one or two hours in this condition of metamorphosis, Michel smeared us again, and quick as thought we resumed our human forms. The salve was given us by our masters; to me it was given by Moyset, to michel by his own master, Guillemin.

As he reported after, "The exhaustion consequent on a werewolf raid was so great that the lycanthropist was often confined to his bed for days, and could hardly move hand or foot, much in the same way as the berserkir and ham rammir in the North were utterly prostrated after their fit had left them."

Pernette Gandillon was a poor girl of Jura, who in 1598 ran about the country on all fours, in the belief that she was a wolf. One day as she was ranging the country in a fit of lycanthropic madness, she came upon two children who were plucking wild strawberries. Filled with a sudden passion for blood, she flew at the little girl and would have brought her down, had not her brother, a lad of four years old, defended her lustily with a knife. Pernette, however, wrenched the weapon from his tiny had, flung him down and gashed his throat, so that he died of the wound. Pernette was torn to pieces by the people in their rage and horror.

Directly after, Pierre, the brother of Pernette Gandillon, was accused of witchcraft. He was charged with having led children to the sabbath, having made hail, and having run about the country in the form of a wolf. The transformation was effected by means of a salve which he had received from the devil. He had on one occasion assumed the form of a hare, but usually he appeared as a wolf, and his skin became covered with shaggy grey hair. He readily acknowledged that the charges brought against him were all well founded, and he allowed that he had, during the period of his transformation, fallen on, and devoured, both beasts and human beings. When he desired to recover his true form, he rolled himself in the dewey grass. His son Georges asserted that he had also been annointed with the salve, and had gone to the sabbath in the shape of a wolf. According to his own testimony, he had fallen upon two goats in one of his expeditions.

The two brothers went mad in prison, running around and acting like animals. Eventually, all three siblings were executed. Thus these became stories of madness and murder more than the occult. The *Codex* insists that Shadowhunters of the time "declared its support for werewolf hunting" in 1612, joining the hysteria (*Codex* 245).

> *Werewolves are not the only shapeshifters among Downworlders, as the volumes in the Institute library attest [in Fallen Angels, p. 175]. Naga are mythical Hindu creatures that can shift from human form to serpent form, and are generally thought of as benevolent (unless they are wronged). Legend has it that they live in secret cities, unseen by humans, and sometimes intermarry with humans; some royal lineages claim descendency from Naga. Naga have achieved demi-god status in Hindu and Buddhism and are immortal; their powers and associations vary with local traditions. Kitsune, another shapeshifter, is rarely seen in its natural fox shape but often in the form of a woman.*
> (Spencer, Kindle Locations 1566-1570)

Selkies too appear on the shelf: they are seals from Scottish folklore who shed their skins and become human, though similar creatures also appear in legends from Alaska.

In fact, man-beast creatures go as far back as we have mythology. One of the world's oldest myths, *The Epic of Gilgamesh*, features the wild beast-man Enkidu, who must be tamed before he can enter civilization. Further, King Gilgamesh refuses the advances of the goddess Ishtar because of her habit of tiring of her lovers and changing them into beasts. He notes:

> *You loved the Shepherd, the Master Herder,*
> *who continually presented you with bread baked*
> *in embers,*
> *and who daily slaughtered for you a kid.*
> *Yet you struck him, and turned him into a wolf,*
> *so his own shepherds now chase him*
> *and his own dogs snap at his shins.*
> (*Epic of Gilgamesh*)

This of course parallels the later Greek myth of Actaeon, whom Artemis transformed into a deer to be killed by his own hunting hounds. The gods frequently transformed people into all manner of animals, including wolves, to punish them. In fact, the word lycanthrope (Greek for wolf-man) comes from the myth of Lycaon. King Lycaon, or possibly his sons, committed heresy by killing a child and serving him for dinner to the god Zeus, who was visiting. Zeus was horrified and transformed the father into a wolf, killing the sons with his lightning bolt. He spared only the youngest, Nyctimus, whom he appointed as the new king and forbade to ever offer human sacrifice. Pausanias, in his second-century travelogue, describes this myth: "Lykaon brought a human baby to the altar of Zeus Lykaios, and sacrificed it, pouring out its blood upon the altar, and according to the legend immediately after the sacrifice he was changed from a man to a wolf." Intriguingly, Pausanias goes on to describe the folk legends that grew from this myth, adding:

> It is said, for instance, that ever since the time of Lykaon a man has changed into a wolf at the sacrifice to Zeus Lykaios, but that the change is not for life; if, when he is a wolf, he abstains from human flesh, after nine years he becomes a man again, but if he tastes human flesh he remains a beast for ever.
>
> (*Pausanias Description of Greece* 2.1–6)

15

Fairies

The fey are not literally the offspring of a demon and an angel. The whole notion of faeries being "half angel and half demon" is not the same as warlocks being half demon. The legend is that faeries were originally created from the union of angels and demons. But every faerie that is alive today (as far as we know) was born the child of other faeries. We don't actually know how the fey were initially created. All we have to work from is the legend. So faeries don't have "demon blood" or "angel blood" in the way that warlocks have an actual direct demon parent or in the way that Jace and Clary have actual angel blood.
(Clare, "Fairies")

In the old folklore, fairies "are said to be of a midle Nature betuixt Man and Angel, as were Dæmons thought to be of old" (Kirk 5). *City of Bones* suggests fairies may be "fallen angels, cast out of heaven for their pride" (104). Indeed, some legends have fairies as a group of angels who refused to support either side in Lucifer's rebellion against God. Thus they were not fit for heaven or hell but a middle path. British fairies live "under the hill" in the burial mounds, so they were originally spirits of the dead or possibly cultural memory of the smaller folk who fought with stone arrows before the arrival of iron. The prohibition against eating fairy food exists because participating in the underworld will bind one to it forever. Of course, iron is a safeguard against fairies – the symbol of civilization and modern technology in contrast with the natural world.

> *Metals, and Iron of the North, (hence the Loadstone causes a tendency to that Point,) by ane Antipathy thereto, these odious far-scenting Creatures shrug and fright at all that comes thence relating to so abhorred a Place, whence their Torment is eather begun, or feared to come hereafter.* (Kirk 14)

Running water and religious tokens – natural barriers and tokens of the civilized world yet again – are said to offer mortals safety. Holly Black adds that fairies have a separate moral system – they laugh at funerals and cry at weddings, as the old tales say (Link and Black). Fairies must speak the truth and will keep any oaths they give, but they are known for being tricky with the exact wording.

> *Do not sign any contracts or agree to any bargains with faeries. Faeries love to haggle but will usually do so only if they are sure they will win. Do not eat or drink anything a faerie gives you. Do not go attend their magical revels under the hills. They will paint a beautiful picture of what awaits you there, but its beauty is false and hollow. Do not*

tease a faerie about their height. Do not expect
direct answers to direct questions. Do expect indi-
rect answers to indirect questions.
(*Codex* 106)

In episode five of the show, "Moo Shu to Go," Isabelle and Jace interrogate Melliorn at his home in Central Park (where his tent is decorated with butterflies because he's in mourning). He carefully responds to every question with another question or a "perhaps" and the pair leave having learned nothing concrete.

Fairies exist in stories around the world, often as former gods remembered from an older time or helpful ancestral spirits. They are the dryads and naiads of Greek myth, Germanic Nixies, Persian Peris, the Hindu, Buddhist, and Jain Yakshas; the Chilean Pillan; the Bediadari of Malaysia; and the Japanese Yōkai, which include kitsune, oni, and other supernatural beings. "The Irish called them the Sidhe, or spirit-race, or the Feadh-Ree, a modification of the word Peri" (Wilde).

"Seers, or Men of the Second Sight, (Fæmales being seldome so qualified) have very terrifying Encounters with them" (Kirk 7-8). Only a few people in British folklore have the Sight and can perceive the hidden world. The same is true in the world of the Shadowhunters. Of course, fairies are most famous for stealing people away – often babies or young lovers.

THE evil influence of the fairy glance does not
kill, but it throws the object into a death-like

*trance, in which the real body is carried off to
some fairy mansion, while a log of wood, or some
ugly, deformed creature is left in its place, clothed
with the shadow of the stolen form. Young
women, remarkable for beauty, young men, and
handsome children, are the chief victims of the
fairy stroke. The girls are wedded to fairy chiefs,
and the young men to fairy queens; and if the
mortal children do not turn out well, they are sent
back, and others carried off in their place. It is
sometimes possible, by the spells of a powerful
fairy-man, to bring back a living being from
Fairy-land. But they are never quite the same
after. They have always a spirit-look, especially if
they have listened to the fairy music. For the fairy
music is soft and low and plaintive, with a fatal
charm for mortal ears.*

(Wilde)

While folktales contribute much of fairy lore, there are also famous ballads such as "Tam Lin" and "Thomas the Rhymer." Both describe the dazzlingly beautiful yet treacherous queen. The former describes a teind or tithe to hell – a person, sacrificed every seven years. The latter has the fairy queen steal a mortal to be her lover and showing him the three paths to Heaven, Hell, and Fairie. Alec references this one as the teens find themselves at the famous three roads (*Heavenly Fire* 353).

*O see ye not that narrow road,
So thick beset with thorns and briers?*

That is the path of righteousness,
Tho after it but few enquires.

And see not ye that braid braid road,
That lies across that lily leven?
That is the path to wickedness,
Tho some call it the road to heaven.

And see not ye that bonny road,
That winds about the fernie brae?
That is the road to fair Elfland,
Where thou and I this night maun gae.

But, Thomas, ye maun hold your tongue,
Whatever ye may hear or see,
For, if you speak word in Elflyn land,
Ye'll neer get back to your ain countrie.
(Child Ballad 37)

Bridget sings this as a further nod to the tradition. Central Park's Turtle Pond is the entrance to their realm in New York, though there are passages to other lands, like Idris and Edom, seem in *City of Heavenly Fire*. Learning a fairy's true name will give one power over them, so a fairy who approaches Tessa at the Lightwood Ball only suggests Tessa call her Hyacinth.

While Jace and his friends visit the Fairy Queen in *City of Ashes*, fairies feature most heavily in the upcoming *Dark Artifices* series. The heroes of the story have two half-fairy siblings – one exiled for her birth, and one stolen by the Wild Hunt.

Their father, when asked about his seven years with a beautiful fairy, would quote the "Belle Dame Sans Merci" by Keats:

> *She took me to her elfin grot,*
> *And there she wept, and sigh'd fill sore,*
> *And there I shut her wild wild eyes*
> *With kisses four.*
> *And there she lullèd me asleep,*
> *And there I dream'd—Ah! woe betide!*
> *The latest dream I ever dream'd*
> *On the cold hill's side.*
> *I saw pale kings and princes too,*
> *Pale warriors, death-pale were they all;*
> *They cried—"La Belle Dame sans Merci*
> *Hath thee in thrall!"*

The story "Pale Kings and Princes" reveals more of what truly happened: A beautiful lady of the Seelie Court lost her heart to the son of an angel. Andrew fell in love as well, and his brother Arthur refused to leave his side. The lady's sister claimed Arthur and tortured him. Andrew's paramour concealed this fact, and she and Arthur lived happily:

> *She gave Andrew a silver chain to wear around his*
> *neck, a token of her love, and she taught him the*
> *ways of the Fair Folk. She danced with him in rev-*
> *els beneath starry skies. She fed him moonshine*
> *and showed him how to give way to the wild.*

Some nights they heard Arthur's screams, and she told him it was an animal in pain, and pain was in an animal's nature.

She did not lie, for she could not lie.

Humans are animals.

Pain is their nature.

When Arthur discovered how his brother was in torment, "The lady thought her lover would go mad with the grief of it and the guilt." She wove him a lie he could choose to believe: "That he had been ensorcelled to love her; that he had never betrayed his brother; that he was only a slave; that these seven years of love had been a lie." She allowed them to escape, and when she could not bear constant reminders of the lover she had lost, she left their two children on Arthur's doorstep. "She had nothing left to live for, then, and so lived no longer….This is how a faerie loves: with her whole body and soul. This is how a faerie loves: with destruction."

When they have a visitor, Jules quotes the other popular fairy poem, Tam Lin, of a human condemned to pay the teind to hell and a mortal women who steals him back from the fairies. "'So first let pass the horses black and then let pass the brown … One robed in black, one brown, one white—it's an official delegation. From the Courts" ("Lady Midnight Excerpt").

Holly Black's trilogy (Tithe, Valient, Ironside) shares several themes and motifs with Clare's: a girl grows up thinking she's human, but as a teenager, she meets a mysterious, irresistible figure and discovers her heritage lies in his world, as does her future. She chooses him, though she adventures with a geeky, male best friend who knows all kinds of science fiction trivia. (Holly Black's character is called Corny, a name that he despairs over as "King of the Dorks.") Though he's actually human and her connection to normality and childhood, he too becomes ensnared in the magical world. In the end, the heroine wins with a clever trick and claims the man she loves as well as her own power.

Both young women, struggling with identity, must face the children they could've been. Clary befriends Isabelle, who grew up in Shadowhunter culture and is an adept warrior, but she also connects with Sebastian, the demon child her father got to raise. Likewise, Kaye travels into the Seelie Court to retrieve the real Kaye – the human girl that was stolen so she, a fairy changeling, could take her place. Like Jace and Simon, Kaye reveals her true identity to her mother and is rejected, but her foster-mother soon relents.

Most of all, fairies aren't nice and sweet, but terribly cruel. The good and evil fairy queens of Black's

*series both torture Roiben to watch him squirm,
and the good one tries to force him to kill his own
sister. Clare's queen likewise makes Jace and Clary
kiss for her entertainment. Worse, both queens
betray the protagonist couple, twisting their bargains.*
(Frankel, Myths and Motifs)

Clare's fairy queen is actually supposed to be the one from
her friend Holly Black's series (Link and Black 179). In those
books, fairies are summoned with a bloody leaf dropped in
the water – Jace likely does this in *City of Ashes*. The *Tithe*
series features a changeling – while not dwelt on extensively,
Clare's series has them as well. The Codex says:

*Because of their isolation and extensive inter-
breeding, faeries risk the weakening of their family
lines. For this reason, faeries spend much of their
time luring humans into their world: either by creating changelings, mundane children taken from
their homes and replaced with a sickly Faerie
child, or by enticing adult humans into their rev-
els. While they trap the adults with them, through
their faerie magic, until they forget their former
lives and "go native", or at least until they can be
used to produce new faerie children, the
changeling mysteriously take on fey attributes and
are able to perform some faerie magic, thus bringing fresh strong blood into the faerie lines.*
(110)

The Clave reluctantly allows this practice as both children are given loving homes.

Fairies are known for the beauty of their world under the hill but also for enticing the unwary to stay forever. The teens use glamors to protect themselves in City of Ashes. Worse yet is the fairy dance, where mortals may stay until they die.

> *If you walk nine times round a fairy rath at the full of the moon, you will find the entrance to the Sifra; but if you enter, beware of eating the fairy food or drinking the fairy wine. The Sidhe will, indeed, wile and draw many a young man into the fairy dance, for the fairy women are beautiful, so beautiful that a man's eyes grow dazzled who looks on them, with their long hair floating like the ripe golden corn and their robes of silver gossamer; they have perfect forms, and their dancing is beyond all expression graceful; but if a man is tempted to kiss a Sighoge, or young fairy spirit, in the dance, he is lost for ever – the madness of love will fall on him, and he will never again be able to return to earth or to leave the enchanted fairy palace. He is dead to his kindred and race for ever more.*
> (Wilde)

After the events of *City of Heavenly Fire,* the Shadowhunters impose sharp sanctions on the fairies – no weapons, no autonomy. The Fairie Courts must pay for all the damaged caused in the Dark War, with brutal reparations. Called the Cold

Peace, it thus has unsavory echoes from world history. The stories of *Shadowhunter Academy* reveal a world of fairies chafing under their harsh punishment, while half-fairy Shadowhunters are cruelly scapegoated. This is a world that echoes Germany before World War II, blamed for all the suffering in a war they only had a small part in. One hopes the Shadowhunters can turn back before the world descends into chaos and slaughter. "Born to Endless Night" has Magnus describing the state of the world:

> *We've been having trouble in New York with faerie fruit sellers as well. Part of the faeries running wild is the Cold Peace itself. People who are not trusted become untrustworthy. But there is something else wrong as well. Faerie is not a land without rules, without rulers. The Queen who was Sebastian's ally has vanished, and there are many dark rumors as to why. None of which I would repeat to the Clave, because they would only impose harsher punishments on the faeries. They become harsher, and the fey wilder, and the hate between both sides grows day by day.*

Likewise, "Faeries aren't protected under the Accords anymore ... It's forbidden to help them, and they're forbidden from contacting Shadowhunters. Only the Scholomance and the Centurions are meant to deal with faeries—and the Consul and Inquisitor." ("Lady Midnight Excerpt"). Shadowhunters are likewise forbidden to give aid to either the

Seelie or the Unseelie Court. *The Dark Artifices* series will do much with the fairy courts and their politics. Clare explains:

> *There is usually one King or Queen of a Court.*
> *Right now the Seelie Court has a Queen, who*
> *we've met, and the Unseelie court has a King, who*
> *we haven't (but will.) The Seelie fey are fond of*
> *rank. The Unseelie fey have a more chaotic soci-*
> *ety, one that is terrifying and totally messed up.*
> *However in both cases there is a monarch — the*
> *Seelie Queen has no children, but the Unseelie*
> *King actually has a lot of kids. Too many, possibly,*
> *for comfort.*
> (Clare, "faeries")

The court is made up of the "gentry" faeries, who tend to look more human. They often have skin of blue, green, or violet and fantastically colored hair. Aside from royalty, there are also knights, and presumably other ranks. The two courts are the Seelie and Unseelie Court – simplified as the light realm and the dark. Other fairies, such as the Wild Hunt, are unaffiliated with both. Clare adds:

> *The faeries are divided into gentry and common*
> *folk. The gentry are knights, kings and queens,*
> *and court members. They look pretty much like*
> *human beings, with the pointed ears and an occa-*
> *sional other odd quality. The common folk are*
> *nixies, pixies, piskies, brownies, selkies, satyrs,*
> *mermaids, kelpies, and just about everything else*

you might run into.
(Clare, "faeries")

In other posts she mentions dryads, boggarts, hobgoblins, and goblins. A peri, a djinn, and an ifrit spy on the group's conversation at Taki's. There's a kelpie at Pandemonium and a phouka at Magnus's party. Jace mentions in *City of Bones* that "Real elves are about eight inches tall. ... Also, they bite." Thus many unearthly creatures can be classified as fairies rather than demons

Djinn

In English literature, their name was changed to genies. However, in the Quran (and other Islamic texts) they inhabit an unseen world beyond the known universe, which fits well with Shadowhunter demonology. They are fashioned of smokeless flame. Traditionally, some are akin to demons, though others can be good, evil, or neutrally benevolent. Because of this affiliation – separate from humanity but parallel, they are closest to fairies, and, indeed, the *Codex* lists them as such.

Goblins

Jessamine fights one of these off with an electrum-edged parasol. When it observes that she's left the path near Rotten Row so it can plant her blood to create "golden vines with diamonds at their tips" she's revolted (*Clockwork Angel* 138).

Thus these are fairyfolk, but of a cruel vicious nature, likely of the Unseelie or dark court.

Mermaids

Mermaids, a resident of Clare's fairy world, appear throughout the world. Pliny the Elder describes nereids (Greek mermaids), noting, "the portion of the body that resembles the human figure is still rough all over with scales" (Book IX, ch. 4). The Philippines have the sirena and siyokoy. Gwragedd annwn seduced men in Wales. Norse myth has nixies. Jengu (Cameroon), kul (Inuit), merrows (Irish), kapa (Japanese), and vodyanoy (Slavic) dwell in other places. Arabella the mermaid is the only fairy who will attend an early discussion of the Accords in "Vampires, Scones, and Edmund Herondale" in 1857. Many more mermaids live in the East River in New York and in Venice, though Jace says they thrive better in fresh, clean water. "What to Buy the Shadowhunter Who Has Everything" follows Pandemonium Enterprises (mundanes who study the Shadow World) and its quest to give a tour of New York Harbor with a view of "nixies, kelpies, mermaids, various and sundry water spirits" (385). Magnus settles matters with his contacts there.

Nixies

Nixies arrive in the East River to save the Shadowhunters in *City of Ashes*. They're summoned by Jace, whom the Queen of Fairie has promised to help. The Nixie is a type of freshwater mermaid who dwells near human communities. She has been said to be completely green, including her skin, hair, and teeth. The Nixie can usually be distinguished from a mermaid because she's shopping in town in the guise of a human woman. However, peeking under her skirt may reveal a fish tail. She also drips fresh water behind her.

Phouka

The Puca or Phouka is a shapechanger from Ireland. It takes animal forms, most often a black horse with golden eyes. If a human mounts it, it will give them a wild ride, though it's not as murderous as its near-cousin, the kelpie. Some folklore has the pooka becoming a hairy bogeyman or a black goat with curling horns.

Satyrs

In *Clockwork Princess* Cecily and Gabriel meet a shopkeeper who is a satyr and a dealer in dirty demon pictures. Gabriel identifies him as being part of the Unseelie Court. These half-goat men hailed from Greek myth, often rambunctious, drunk, and tricky, but not especially evil. They could be considered the dark side of fairy culture.

16

Bible, Myth, and Other Lore

*With Dante and the Bible – and Paradise Lost,
which is another big influence on these particular
books – these are all works of (for want of a better
term) Christian mythology, specifically the myth
of the Nephilim, and of the war in Heaven, angels
vs. demons, the fall of Lucifer, all of that. And
when you're dealing with a magic system depen-
dent on the idea of angels and demons, you have
to draw on all that, that's your canon.*
("Interview: Cassandra Clare")

Thus the Bible and related texts create much of the Shadowhunter myth and lore. Shadowhunters are tied with religion so completely that the two cannot be clearly separated –
temples, synagogues, and churches support them with caches
of weapons and Jace asks entry to a church "in the name
of the Battle the Never Ends" (*City of Bones*). As he tells
Clary, "all religions assist us in battle" (*City of Bones*). Simi-
larly, Jem describes religious texts as "instruction manuals" for
the Shadowhunters (*Clockwork Prince* 91). Jace quotes "Mea
Culpa" out of the Mass, and Jem quotes the Biblical Song of

Songs, when describing the runes from a Shadowhunter wedding: "Set me as a seal upon thine heart, as a seal upon thine arm; for love is strong as death; jealousy is cruel as the grave" (8:6). Shadowhunters part with the word *Mizpah*, from the story of Laban, quoting the Bible passage: "And Mizpah; for he said, The Lord watch between me and thee, when we are absent one from another" (Genesis 31:49).

City of Glass's Chapter Sixteen is called "Articles of Faith." Meanwhile, Chapter Twelve: "De Profundis" is Latin for "out of the depths," as Clare explains: "Psalm 130 is known as 'De Profundis;' it begins "'Out of the depths have I cried unto thee, O Lord'" ("City of Glass Chapter Titles").

In her other series, "Thirty Pieces of Silver" is, fittingly, the *Clockwork Angel* chapter where Nate betrays his sister. *Clockwork Prince*'s Chapter Twenty-One is "Coals of Fire." Clary adds: "I guess if you're paying a lot of attention you'll recognize this as part of something Jace quotes in *City of Fallen Angels*. Endings, beginnings, new characters, and, I promise, not too bad of a cliffhanger" ("Clockwork Prince Cover and Chapter Titles"). The Bible quote is a reference to turnabout – at last Will reveals his secret of why he's rejected Tessa at the worst possible moment.

Throughout the series, the Bible and the larger body of religious commentary serve as a guide for a world of angels, demons, and heavenly protections. Thus exploring these texts reveals much about the series and its creatures.

Adamas

Adamas is material given to the Shadowhunters by the Angel Raziel, silver-white and translucent. It is used for the demon towers, steles, seraph blades, and other weapons to fight the forces of evil.

> *Adamas comes from a word that in classical Latin was used to describe a very hard, incorruptible material and in ancient Greek meant invincible, suitable for the name of the material that makes weapons wielded by Shadowhunters. In Gnosticism, Adamas is a "divine prototype" for the first man, Adam. The word is also used as a term for a kind of spiritual element that radiates from God.* (Spencer, Kindle Locations 1894-1896)

God created man from "dust," but many see it as an original building material – the source of heaven.

The Book of Raziel

After Adam's expulsion from the Garden of Eden, Adam remembered the letters of the Holy Name. As he told his family, "By the light of all luminaries, rule in righteousness and in reverence of Elohim [God]. Also, hold dominion over the spirit and over violence and over misfortune and adversaries rising up over men and women. It is written, be summoned as you wish and desire" (*Sefer Rezial* 3). Using the name of God, he and his descendants performed miracles. As he was dying, he prayed to God for compassion and grace. He added:

> *Grant me knowledge and understanding, that I may know what shall befall me, and my posterity, and all the generations that come after me, and what shall befall me on every day and in every month, and mayest Thou not withhold from me the help of Thy servants and of Thy angels.*
> (Ginzberg)

Three days later, the angel Raziel came with a book in his hand. The angel addressed Adam thus:

> *O Adam, why art thou so fainthearted? Why art thou distressed and anxious? Thy words were heard at the moment when thou didst utter thy supplication and entreaties, and I have received the charge to teach thee pure words and deep understanding, to make thee wise through the contents of the sacred book in my hand, to know what will happen to thee until the day of thy death. And all thy descendants and all the later generations, if they will but read this book in purity, with a devout heart and a humble mind, and obey its precepts, will become like unto thee. They, too, will foreknow what things shall happen, and in what month and on what day or in what night. All will be manifest to them – they will know and understand whether a calamity will*

*come, a famine or wild beasts, floods or drought;
whether there will be abundance of grain or
dearth; whether the wicked will rule the world;
whether locusts will devastate the land; whether
the fruits will drop from the trees unripe; whether
boils will afflict men; whether wars will prevail, or
diseases or plagues among men and cattle;
whether good is resolved upon in heaven, or evil;
whether blood will flow, and the death-rattle of
the slain be heard in the city. And now, Adam,
come and give heed unto what I shall tell thee
regarding the manner of this book and its holiness."*
(Ginzberg)

As the legend tells:

*It is the book out of which all things worth know-
ing can be learnt, and all mysteries, and it teaches
also how to call upon the angels and make them
appear before men, and answer all their questions.
But not all alike can use the book, only he who is
wise and God-fearing, and resorts to it in holiness.
Such a one is secure against all wicked counsels,
his life is serene, and when death takes him from
this world, he finds repose in a place where there
are neither demons nor evil spirits, and out of the
hands of the wicked he is quickly rescued.*
(Ginzberg)

In the thirteenth century, a spellbook called The Book of Raziel appeared, drawing heavily on Kabbalah, the teachings of Jewish mysticism. It contains a detailed angelology, instructions for creating protective amulets with the runes of God's name, and other ancient lore. The *Codex* mentions "a distorted version" with "a strange amalgam of kabbalistic teachings, angelology, glosses on the Jewish creation stories, and corrupted forms of demonic incantation," though in a fannish twist on the real history, adds that the runes don't work (119). Nonetheless, the book and the legends around it form some of the background for the Shadowhunters. Clare notes:

> *Raziel, for instance, is an angel from the Jewish kabbalistic tradition, who is supposed to have given Adam, in the Garden of Eden, a book of wisdom – he is sometimes called the Angel of Secrets, or Angel of Knowledge. Therefore he seemed the right angel to have given the Gray Book to the first Shadowhunter.*
> (FAQ)

According to legend, the other angels grew jealous of Adam and threw the Book of Raziel into the ocean, though God took pity on mankind and sent it back to them. Enoch, Noah, and Solomon each used its wisdom in turn.

> *Said Rabbi Eleazar: "In the days of Enos [Enoch], men were deeply versed in occult knowledge and magical science and the manipulation of natural forces, in which no one was more skilled than he,*

since the time of Adam whose chief study was on the occult properties of the leaves of the Tree of Knowledge of good and evil. It was Enos that taught and imparted this occult lore to his contemporaries...Whilst Enos lived, men became initiated into the higher life, as scripture states. 'Then began men to make invocations in the name of Jehovah.'"
(de Manhar 238)

There are other ties between the classic Book of Raziel and the Shadowhunter legacy:

The Book of Raziel has a section of gematria, a mystical math applied to the Bible. In Hebrew, each of the 22 letters has a numeric value, so each word likewise has a value. For instance, eighteen is lucky in Judaism, because it is the numeric value of the word chai, meaning life. (ch has a value of eight, ay has a value of ten). This word magic is an ancient part of Judaism, used to interpret some of the Bible's hidden meanings. At the same time, it's linked to rune magic, the individual magic and meaning of letters. It is written: "The letters are prominent, illuminated by shining lights and complete. Thus, before the creation of the universe, letters are prominent" (Sefer Rezial 55). They are the building blocks of the universe, tools for invoking miracles. In itself, this is quite similar to Clare's rune magic: the letter has a

meaning, power, and story. With the letter shin,
one can "create fire."
(Frankel)

Dante

Tessa and Will begin *Clockwork Angel* and their first meeting arguing whether the ninth circle of Hell is hot or cold – a Dante reference. Indeed, Dante's *Inferno* gives us our modern vision of Hell, with its nine circles, each devoted to punishing a different type of sin. *City of Glass*'s Chapter Fourteen is called "In the Dark Forest" in a reference to the beginning of Dante's *Inferno*. "I found myself within a forest dark." Clare explains that "the narrator, Dante, wanders in a dark forest of confusion and grief" and her characters do as well ("City of Glass Chapter Titles").

Further, the original trilogy echoes Dante's three books as Clary descends into the frightening city of bones, much like hell. The second, like purgatory, has her forced to be Jace's sister, in constant agony. The third book takes her to paradise – Idris, the city of glass. Even Raziel's lesson to Jonathan Shadowhunter: "To destroy the things of darkness, it is sometimes necessary to descend into the shadows to join them" (*Codex* 236) relates, as do signs warning "easy is the descent."

At the end of *City of Fallen Angels*, Jace tells Clary how he loves her:

> *It's a bit of the very last verse from Paradiso –*
> *Dante's Paradise. "My will and my desire were*
> *turned by love, the love that moves the sun and*

the other stars." Dante was trying to explain faith,
I think, as an overpowering love, and maybe it's
blasphemous, but that's how I think of the way I
love you. You came into my life and suddenly I
had one truth to hold on to – that I loved you, and
you loved me.
(407-408)

Edom

When the teens plan to breach the demonic realm of Edom,
Alec quotes the Bible, describing it:

And the streams of Edom shall be turned into
pitch, and her soil into sulfur; her land shall
become burning pitch. Night and day it shall not
be quenched; its smoke shall go up forever. From
generation to generation it shall lie waste; none
shall pass through it forever and ever.
(Isaiah 34:9-10)

It's another realm beyond earth, one of demons and despair.
The land they discover is indeed a burned wasteland. When
they reach its world's Idris, they find that it paralleled earth's
history with another Jonathan Shadowhunter, though he
failed to unite his people against the demons. The demons
took over the land and destroyed it. It is the realm of
Asmodeus and his demonic children, so he has increased
powers, and the Shadowhunters' runes have less. Lilith rules

beside Asmodeus, so Asmodeus allows Sebastian to wreak havoc there. Sebastian plots to rule this land and be king over hell, as he thinks, but he's thwarted in his quest.

Faustus

Magnus summons Azazel with the Latin demonic invocation that comes from Marlowe's Dr. Faustus. As Faustus adds in the play:

> *Within this circle is Jehovah's name,*
> *Forward and backward anagrammatiz'd,*
> *Th' abbreviated names of holy saints,*
> *Figures of every adjunct to the heavens,*
> *And characters of signs and erring [29] stars,*
> *By which the spirits are enforc'd to rise.*
> (I:iii:lns 25-29)

With his protective circle in place, inscribed with God's name over and over and symbols of saints and the stars, he feels secure. He then calls on Mephistophilis in Latin with the following invocation:

> *Sint mihi dii Acherontis propitii! Valeat numen triplex Jehovoe! Ignei, aerii, aquatani spiritus, salvete! Orientis princeps Belzebub, inferni ardentis monarcha, et Demogorgon, propitiamus vos, ut appareat et surgat Mephistophilis Dragon, quod tumeraris: per Jehovam, Gehennam, et consecratam aquam quam nunc spargo, signumque*

crucis quod nunc facio, et per vota nostra, ipse
nunc surgat nobis dicatus Mephistophilis!
(I:iii:lns 30-31)

Folklore

Several stories of Europe are blended into the lore. Isaac Laquedem, an antlered warlock, is also known from the French folktale of the Wandering Hunter, according to the *Codex*. It calls him one of the eight living warlocks who claim to have been born earlier than Jonathan Shadowhunter. The *Codex* also lists the Crusades, the witch trials, Transylvania in 1450, and St. Patrick's battle against snakes (but also demons) as part of Shadowhunter history (*Codex* 240).

Brothers Grimm

Even the Brothers Grimm have their place in Shadowhunter lore: Certainly, they offer many tales of men encountering demons or fairies and having to trick or bargain their way free. Much of our concepts of bargains with demons or laws of fairyland come from popular folklore.

> *"The year was 1828," Balogh declaimed. "This was*
> *before the Accords, mind you, before the Down-*
> *worlders were brought into line and taught to be*
> *civilized."*

> *Out of the corner of his eye, Simon saw their his-*
> *tory lecturer stiffen. It didn't seem wise to offend a*

warlock, even one as seemingly unflappable as Catarina Loss, but Balogh continued unheeded.

"Europe was in chaos. Unruly revolutionaries were fomenting discord across the continent. And in the German states, a small cabal of warlocks took advantage of the political situation to visit the most unseemly miseries upon the local population. Some of you mundanes may be familiar with this time of tragedy and havoc from the tales told by the Brothers Grimm." At the surprised look on several students' faces, Balogh smiled for the first time. "Yes, Wilhelm and Jacob were in the thick of it. Remember, children, all the stories are true."

As Simon tried to wrap his head around the idea that there might, somewhere in Germany, be a large bean stalk with an angry giant at the top, Balogh continued his story. He told the class of the small band of Shadowhunters that had been dispensed to "deal with" the warlocks. Of their journey into a dense German forest, its trees alive with dark magic, its birds and beasts enchanted to defend their territory against the forces of justice. In the dark heart of the forest, the warlocks had summoned a Greater Demon, planning to unleash its might on the people of Bavaria.
("The Lost Herondale")

What follows is like a fairy tale indeed, with love, death and immutable consequences for those who prove themselves unworthy.

Heavenly Fire

Jace quotes the Song of Moses (Deuteronomy 32: 22) to explain to Clary the heavenly fire that burns in him: "For a fire is kindled by my anger, and it burns to the depths of Sheol, devours the earth and its increase, and sets on fire the foundations of the mountains." God's heavenly wrath was known for burning the unrighteous, and the Angel Raziel sends this fire to Jace in the Archangel Michael's sword. Later Raphael adds that the heavenly fire resembles God's pillar of fire, with which he guided the Israelites in the desert (*Heavenly Fire* 460).

Idris

Idris is a Welsh name. It means "ardent lord," from udd (lord) + ris (enthusiastic). Thus the mountain Cadair Idris is Idris' Chair, seat of a legendary hero. It is said to offer either madness or poetic inspiration to whoever spends a night at its summit, and Will travels here in search of Tessa in *Clockwork Princess*. "Idris the Giant" (c. 560–c. 632) was a king of Meirionnydd in early medieval Wales and a noted astronomer.

In the Qur'an, Idris is a prophet, usually identified with Enoch. Of course, Idris, home of the Shadowhunters, has logical links with the prophet Enoch, as his Book of Enoch is the source of much of their lore including the story of Raziel.

Likewise, it is a realm of heroes as well as legends, poetry, and madness.

Iratze

The healing and pain-killing rune is the iratze – likely the most common rune in the series. The healing rune is actually a nickname or title for the Virgin Mary in the Basque or Spanish languages. Thus it connects with her as a source of intersession, comfort and restoration.

Magic Swords and Grails

The Cup and its choices are numinous magic and part of a long tradition of the concept of magic that is based on or requires specific personal attributes from the magic user. What makes someone worthy of Excalibur? Worthy of Thor's Hammer? Of passing the Sphinx? Check out http://tvtropes.org/pmwiki/pmwiki.php/Main/ OnlyTheWorthyMayPass for examples of this. It simply has something to do with the nature of the person contradicting the nature of the magic. If anyone knew what made someone unworthy of Ascension, they wouldn't let them try for it. Caterina's theory is that it's random and that it exists to make sure that the people who try for Ascension are willing to risk their lives to become Shad-

owhunters.

("Major Spoilers for Angels Twice Descending")

Certainly Ascension is a life-or-death test of worthiness...though the criteria is uncertain. The cup and the spiritual test it offers echo the grail of Arthurian lore. Clare's consideration of worthiness shows up several times – especially with the hero swords Cortana and the Sword of Heavenly Fire, which tests people by impaling them.

Before all this came the Mortal Instruments: Jonathan Shadowhunter reportedly dreams of pledging his sword to the Crusades and standing "in blazing sunlight, golden like the light of heaven, and my sword shone so that I myself was blinded" (*Codex* 233). After this, under demon attack, he prays for protection and Raziel brings him the Mortal Instruments. The heavy-bladed silver sword Maellartach has a hilt shaped like outspread wings. Its alliance is seraphic – Magnus describes it as a thousand times stronger than the angel blades since its power comes from Raziel himself (*City of Glass* 141). It tests people as well, forcing Shadowhunters to speak the truth and tearing it out of them. Likewise, Clary draws the cup from its hiding place and locates the mirror. Clare adds:

> *The Mortal Sword is one in a long line of fictional,*
> *historical and mythological swords. There are*
> *swords so famous we all know their names –*
> *Arthur had Excalibur, Roland had Durendal,*
> *Caesar had Crocea Mors, and Siegfried had Bal-*
> *mung (made by Wayland Smith), etc. I wanted*
> *the Mortal Sword to be one of history's famous*

swords, so, since the MI series draws on a lot of Biblical myth, Maellartach is supposed to be the sword in Genesis – "So God placed at the east of the garden of Eden Cherubims, and a flaming sword which turned every way, to keep the way of the tree of life." So it's the sword that separates man from Paradise, in theory. It's also why I named one of the chapters in Ashes East of Eden.
(Reader's Quill)

A second sword that appears in *City of Lost Souls* is Glorious, the sword of Joshua. The series describes the sword of heavenly fire as the one given to Joshua in this story from the Bible:

And it came to pass, when Joshua was by Jericho, that he lifted up his eyes and looked, and, behold, there stood a man over against him with his sword drawn in his hand: and Joshua went unto him, and said unto him, Art thou for us, or for our adversaries? And he said, Nay; but as captain of the host of the LORD am I now come. And Joshua fell on his face to the earth, and did worship, and said unto him, What saith my lord unto his servant? And the captain of the LORD'S host said unto Joshua, Loose thy shoe from off thy foot; for the place whereon thou standest is holy. And Joshua did so.
(Joshua 5: 13-15)

The Archangel Michael gave Joshua his own sword, and with it, Joshua led his army against Jericho and won the day. Simon receives this sword from the Angel Raziel and gives it to Clary, demonstrating that they are both in heaven's favor and can strike down their enemies. For both it is a moment of triumph: Simon gives Clary the sword "and in that moment, she was no longer Clary, his friend since childhood, but a Shadowhunter, an avenging angel who belonged with that sword in her hand" (*Lost Souls* 485-486).

In Idris, she finds Heosphoros, a family sword of the Morgenstern family and the smaller match to Phaesphoros. The latter is the sword of Sebastian, one of force and brutality that Clary must match with subtle quickness. Diana Wrayburn gives her Heosphoros "dawn-bringer" and encourages her to return honor to the Morgensterns with it – another worthiness test. She indeed returns light and hope to the Shadowhunters by using it in the end.

Finally, Elias Carstairs, Jem's uncle, inherits the sword Cortana, which eventually goes to Emma, heroine of *The Dark Artifices*. According to legend, Cortana was the sword of Ogier the Dane, "cut down" (hence the name) from the sword of the Arthurian hero Tristan. It bore the inscription "My name is Cortana, of the same steel and temper as Joyeuse and Durendal." Durendal is the hero's sword in *The Song of Roland*, while Joyeuse belonged to Charlemagne. Wayland the Smith made Excalibur and Joyeuse – Arthur and Lancelot's swords, as well as Roland's Durendal (*Heavenly Fire* 5).

The Mark of Cain

Cain, who killed his brother Abel out of jealousy, is the world's first murderer – in several series, vampires are descended from Cain or bear the mark of Cain, providing an interesting link between concepts. Genesis 4:11-16 depicts Cain's punishment when the Lord discovers Cain's crime:

> *And now art thou cursed from the earth, which hath opened her mouth to receive thy brother's blood from thy hand; When thou tillest the ground, it shall not henceforth yield unto thee her strength; a fugitive and a vagabond shalt thou be in the earth. And Cain said unto the Lord, My punishment is greater than I can bear. Behold, thou hast driven me out this day from the face of the earth; and from thy face shall I be hid; and I shall be a fugitive and a vagabond in the earth; and it shall come to pass, that every one that findeth me shall slay me. And the LORD said unto him, Therefore whosoever slayeth Cain, vengeance shall be taken on him sevenfold. And the LORD set a mark upon Cain, lest any finding him should kill him.*

Cain is banished from his family, cursed to be a "fugitive" and "vagabond" or "wanderer." At the same time, the mark is a sign of mercy – Cain is banished yet protected for no one else to kill.

*Simon, as a vampire who can walk in the sun, has
not sinned. He bit an angel, but only after the
angel, Jace, offered his blood freely. Yet Rafael
wants to kill him as an "abomination." In fact,
thanks to the angel blood, he has become something new. Like Cain, he finds that everyone, from
the Shadowhunters of Idris to the vampires, wants
to kill him. He is no longer part of human society,
and Rafael reminds him that Simon cannot pre-
tend to be a human teen and continue to live with
his mother. He, like Cain, has become set apart.
Clary gives him the protection and curse that God
gave Cain – a warning for others to leave his punishment to a higher power. Ironically, Simon's
curse makes him the only one able to summon
Raziel.*

(Frankel)

Chapter Three of *City of Fallen Angels* is called "Sevenfold."
On her blog, Clare quotes the Bible: "And the Lord said unto
him, Therefore whosoever slayeth Cain, vengeance shall be
taken on him sevenfold. And the Lord set a mark upon Cain,
lest any finding him should kill him. Well, that whole Mark
of Cain business wasn't just going to go away." As she adds for
"Chapter Seventeen: Cain Rose Up":

*And Cain talked with Abel his brother: and it
came to pass, when they were in the field, that
Cain rose up against Abel his brother, and slew
him. All of this stuff is from Genesis 4, the Cain*

and Abel story — it's thematically called up throughout the book since it's a story about family, murder, sin, forgiveness and blood.
("City of Fallen Angels Chapter Titles")

Mene Mene Tekel Upharsin

Belshazzar the king made a great feast to a thousand of his lords, and drank wine before the thousand... Then they brought the golden vessels that were taken out of the temple of the house of God which was at Jerusalem; and the king, and his princes, his wives, and his concubines, drank in them. They drank wine, and praised the gods of gold, and of silver, of brass, of iron, of wood, and of stone. In the same hour came forth fingers of a man's hand, and wrote over against the candlestick upon the plaister of the wall of the king's palace: and the king saw the part of the hand that wrote. Then the king's countenance was changed, and his thoughts troubled him, so that the joints of his loins were loosed, and his knees smote one against another. The king cried aloud to bring in the astrologers, the Chaldeans, and the soothsayers. And the king spake, and said to the wise men of Babylon, Whosoever shall read this writing, and shew me the interpretation thereof, shall be clothed with scarlet, and have a chain of gold about his neck, and shall be the third ruler in the kingdom.

The wise men of the kingdom tried, but only Daniel, a Jew, succeeded. He told the king:

> "This is the inscription that was written: mene, mene, tekel, parsin. "Here is what these words mean: Mene: God has numbered the days of your reign and brought it to an end. Tekel: You have been weighed on the scales and found wanting. Peres: Your kingdom is divided and given to the Medes and Persians."
> (Daniel 5: 1-28).

Basically, the four words explain, "God has decided to end your reign of tyranny, and other nations will come to destroy you." When Clary tears open the ship in *City of Ashes,* Valentine sees her rune this way – a prophet has come to topple him from his throne. Clary also writes this message in the sand when she defeats Valentine, emphasizing that God has sent her to end his reign.

The Nephilim's way of life does end thanks to Valentine, as the Downworlders unite and earn Council seats by fighting against him. *City of Glass's* chapter twenty: "Weighed in the Balance," is from this: "You are weighed in the balance, and found wanting." In the third book, Jace tells Simon that Clary's amazing rune gifts are a portent – "The Laws are changing. The old ways may never be the right ways again" (*City of Glass* 60).

Nephilim

"We are sometimes called the Nephilim," said Hodge. "In the Bible they were the offspring of humans and angels. The legend of the origin of Shadowhunters is that they were created more than a thousand years ago, when humans were being overrun by demon invasions from other worlds. A warlock summoned the Angel Raziel, who mixed some of his own blood with the blood of men in a cup, and gave it to those men to drink. Those who drank the Angel's blood became Shadowhunters, as did their children and their children's children."
(*City of Bones*)

Clare took the term from the Bible, using it to describe her own angel-born creations.

The original Bible passage is brief: "There were giants in the earth in those days; and also after that, when the sons of God came in unto the daughters of men, and they bare children to them, the same became mighty men which were of old, men of renown" (Genesis 6:4). In this Bible quote, the Hebrew word for "sons of God," Nephilim, has sparked much debate– are they angels who had children with human women? The descendants Adam and Eve meeting the descendants of another tribe? Many modern works suggest they're fallen angels, angels who strayed from heaven for the joys of life on earth.

The puzzling word appears again later when Joshua and his followers describe Canaan as a place of "giants." The Hebrew word *gibbowr*, literally meaning "powerful, warrior, tyrant, giant or mighty man," was used often to describe descendants of various nephilim, Thus nephilim appear as mighty warriors, supernatural heroes, and fallen angels across different texts.

As Henry Branwell points out in *The Infernal Devices* trilogy, Nephilim in the Bible may not be monsters, as there's "an issue of translation from the original Aramaic" (*Clockwork Angel* 140). The Bible has of course been translated many times to create, say, the King James version, so some of the nuances are lost. In the *Book of Enoch*, the Angel Uriel condemns them, calling them, "the angels who have connected themselves with women, and their spirits assuming many different forms are defiling mankind and shall lead them astray into sacrificing to demons [and worshipping them]" (19:1). Some tales consider them mighty wielders of magic, who called on God to give them power. Enoch, a Biblical figure so righteous that God carried him straight to heaven, had magic, but this was beyond the Nephilim. As the Zohar, the book of Jewish mysticism states:

> *All the just men who lived subsequent to Enos*
> *[Enoch], as Jared, Methusalah and Henoch, did*
> *all in their power to restrain the practice of magi-*
> *cal arts, but their efforts proved futile and ineffec-*
> *tual; so that the professors of them, proud of their*
> *occult knowledge, became rebellious and disobedi-*
> *ent to their Lord, saying, 'Who is Shaddai [one of*

God's many names], the almighty, that we should serve him and what profit should we have in praying unto Him'?' Thus spake they and foolishly imagined that by their occultism and magic they would be able to nullify and turn away the oncoming judgment that was to sweep them wholly out of existence. Beholding their wicked deeds and practices, the Holy One caused the earth to revert back to its former condition and become immersed in water. After the deluge, however, He gave the earth again to mankind, promising, in His mercy, it should never again and in like manner be destroyed. It is written, 'The Lord caused the earth to be covered with the deluge' (Psalms xxix:10). The word for Lord, here, is Jehovah and not Alhim; the first representing mercy, the other severity and judgment. In the time of Enos, even young children became students and trained in the higher mysteries and knowledge of the secret doctrine."
(de Manhar 238)

These practitioners of magic were the Nephilim, the ones God sent Noah's flood to destroy. Raziel announces that the Shadowhunters will be of men and of angels together, incorporating all these legends (*Codex* 237).

Norse Myth

Valentine's ravens are named for Odin's: "Hugin and Munin were Valentine's pet birds. Their names mean 'Thought' and 'Memory,'" Luke explains (*City of Bones*). This casts him as the father-god of his imagined universe, though he's closer to rebellious Loki. Ash is a sacred wood in the series for Yggdrasil, the world tree (*Codex* 26). Like the *Mortal Instruments,* Norse myth too has epics of magic swords and great deeds ... and also the story of Siegmund, with brother-sister incest.

Ourobouros

Ouroboros (Greek for tail-devourer) is a symbol with a snake, sometimes two, swallowing each other's tails. Will comments it means "the end of the world and the beginning" in alchemy (*Clockwork Angel* 5). It's a symbol of endless rebirth, likely inspiring the modern infinity symbol. It's seen in Greek alchemic texts, the Egyptian Book of the Dead, European woodcuts, Mithran mystery cults, Norse world serpent myths, Native American art, and around the world in Japan, India, and the lands of the Aztecs. It has been associated with the Roman two-faced god Janus, the Chinese Ying Yang, and the Biblical serpent. In the second century *Chrysopoeia of Cleopatra* its black and white halves represent the Gnostic duality of existence, like yin-yang. Will notes the tail devourer is also "an ancient alchemical symbol meant to represent the different dimensions –our world, inside the serpent, and the rest of existence, outside" (*Clockwork Angel* 85).

Henry describes the ourobouros as "The symbol of the containment of demon energies" (*Clockwork Princess* 438). It's the symbol of the Dark Sisters and The Magister, controller of demons. It's also printed on each Pyxis box. Edmund Herondale keeps one that holds the spirit of the first demon he slew at age fourteen, but his young son Will finds it and opens it, killing his sister and destroying his own life.

Parabatai

When asked, James Carstairs explains that Greek Parabatai are a pair of warriors – one soldier and one chariot driver. For Nephilim, they are "a matched team of warriors – two men who swear to protect each other and guard each other's backs" (*Clockwork Angel* 209). In Shadowhunter lore, David and Jonathan in the Bible had such a relationship. In the story, Jonathan's father, King Saul, schemed against David, but Jonathan stood by him nonetheless.

> *And it came to pass, when he had made an end of speaking unto Saul, that the soul of Jonathan was knit with the soul of David, and Jonathan loved him as his own soul. And Saul took him that day, and would let him go no more home to his father's house. Then Jonathan and David made a covenant, because he loved him as his own soul.*
> (1 Samuel 18: 1-3)

They are held up as a famous example of perfect platonic love and partnership. As Jem explains, "Their souls were knit together by Heaven, and out of that Jonathan Shadowhunter took the idea of parabatai" (*Clockwork Princess* 325). Jonathan Shadowhunter coincidentally had a best friend named David. From the Biblical tradition, Jonathan invented the parabatai bond for them. Far later, David and his followers became the first Silent Brothers, and he parted from his best friend, much as Will and Jem do later on.

The oath that parabatai take also comes from the Bible: Naomi, an Israelite, leaves Moab to return home after the death of her husband and sons. Her daughter-in-law, Ruth, wanted to follow her to that land for love of her, to bear children that ritually would take their place, but Naomi refused.

> *And Ruth said, Entreat me not to leave thee, and*
> *to return from following after thee, for whither*
> *thou goest, I will go; and where thou lodgest, I will*
> *lodge; thy people shall be my people, and thy God*
> *my God; where thou diest, will I die, and there*
> *will I be buried: The Lord do so to me, and more*
> *also, if aught but death part thee and me.*
> (Ruth 1:16-17)

With "the angel" substituted for the Lord, this is the Parabatai oath, shown at the end of *Clockwork Prince*. Will references this story as he insists he will stay with a dying Jem no matter what. While their devotion to each other is truly perfect, to the point of a love triangle free of jealousy, Julian and Emma will have an equally significant one in the series to come.

Other important pairs include Jace and Alec as well as former parabatai Valentine and Luke, whose devotion has turned to hatred. All the pairs offer contrasting personalities bound in mutual care and protection. Clare comments, "I tend to think with every pair of parabatai there's one that grounds the other – Jem grounds Will, Alec grounds Jace, and Julian grounds Emma" ("Blackthorns and Co").

To pass the Fiery Trial and become permanent partners, the pair enter a "Venn diagram of fire" and are bound there. "It wasn't symbolic. The parabatai test is the test of fire," the warlock Catarina says. "You stand in rings of fire to make your bond. This ... this is the test of water. The nature of the test requires that you have no knowledge of the test. Mentally preparing for the test can affect the outcome." When she gives them the test of water, Clary and Simon discover they link mentally and find each other even in hallucinations. Jem notes this and quotes, "And it came to pass that the soul of Jonathan was knit with the soul of David, and Jonathan loved him as his own soul." ("The Fiery Trial")

Paradise Lost

And there was war in heaven: Michael and his angels fought against the dragon; and the dragon fought and his angels, And prevailed not; neither was their place found any more in heaven. And the great dragon was cast out, that old serpent, called the Devil, and Satan, which deceiveth the whole world: he was cast out into the earth, and

his angels were cast out with him.
(Revelations 12:7-9)

Milton's *Paradise Lost* famously dramatizes the fall of the angels as Lucifer leads a massive rebellion against God. The following lines from the poem begin *City of Bones*:

I sung of Chaos and eternal Night;
Taught by the heavenly Muse to venture down
The dark descent, and up to re-ascend,
(3:18-20)

This famous poem has a heavy influence on the series – Valentine lives by Lucifer's creed of "Better to rule in hell than serve in Heaven." Idris appears heaven and he is its Lucifer, leading its citizens in rebellion to create a new more powerful world. Valentine, like Lucifer, is descended from angels and given the mission to protect humanity. He even insists that the Shadowhunters are "the closest thing that exists in this world to gods" (*Ashes* 262). In one scene, he brags of his falling star crest and his name Morgan-stern, morning star (Lucifer's star) and then quotes the Bible: "How art thou fallen from heaven, O Lucifer, son of the morning! How art thou cut down to the ground, which didst weaken the nations!" (Isaiah 14:12). Sebastian too "looked like the sort of bad angel who might have followed Lucifer out of heaven" (*Glass* 452).

Of course, this is the story of Valentine after his
fall – every time he's mentioned in the series it's as

> *a monster – the murderer of the innocent who*
> *tried to start a genocidal war. Clare's first trilogy is*
> *the story of Valentine's quest to climb back from*
> *hiding and claim the power of the angel Raziel in*
> *a second rebellion against the Clave. Paradise Lost*
> *is a similar story – Lucifer begins it cast down to*
> *hell, surrounded by his defeated followers. How-*
> *ever, pride and hate fill him until he's determined*
> *to take power.*
> (Frankel)

Valentine made Jace read *Paradise Lost* over and over as a child and comments that Milton's devil is far more interesting than his God (*Ashes* 258). Valentine was clearly grooming Jace for a special place in his army. Satan describes how Lucifer has fallen:

> *But O how fall'n! how chang'd*
> *From him, who in the happy Realms of Light*
> *Cloth'd with transcendent brightness didst out-*
> *shine*
> *Myriads though bright*
> (1:84-88)

Valentine is banished like Lucifer and loses everything – wife, family, followers, status. In Paradise Lost, when Satan sees how they've fallen, he proposes they destroy the gloating foe, either by strength or by guile.

In Arms not worse, in foresight much advanc't,
We may with more successful hope resolve
To wage by force or guile eternal Warr
Irreconcileable, to our grand Foe,
Who now triumphs, and in th' excess of joy
Sole reigning holds the Tyranny of Heav'n.
(1:119-124)

Thus Valentine plans to win by guile as he sends Sebastian to Idris to charm the Shadowhunters and destroy the wards while he sets himself up as the Clave's focus.

City of Glass's "Chapter Eleven: All the Host of Hell" comes from the Milton quote: "The hollow abyss/ Heard far and wide, and all the host of hell/ With deafening shout returned them loud acclaim" ("City of Glass Chapter Titles"). Later, Magnus, himself the child of a demon, notes, "I look at Alec and I feel like Lucifer in *Paradise Lost*. 'Abashed the Devil stood, And felt how awful goodness is." (*Heavenly Fire* 429).

Religious Fundamentalism

Valentine's sacrificing his son in *City of Glass* mirrors the Binding of Isaac but is done for more selfish reasons. When Valentine insists to Raziel that his sacrifice was righteous, Raziel disdainfully retorts that God doesn't want him to sacrifice his child – this is the actual point of the Bible story, in which God demands Abraham's son but ends by accepting a ram in its place. "You dream only of your own glory," says Raziel, "and you do not love heaven."

Obviously, Valentine's quest against the Downworlders takes on qualities of Nazism, with his belief that the other races are corrupted and evil. It's Clary and her friends who reject these beliefs and save the world.

Silent Brothers

Nate calls the Silent Brothers "the Gregori" (*Clockwork Angel* 277). The Grigori (from Greek egrgoroi, "The Watchers") are, in some versions of lore, the fallen angels who mated with mortal women and birthed the Biblical Nephilim described in Genesis 6:4. However, some traditions of Italian witchcraft describe angelic Grigori that appear in the books of Enoch and Jubilees. In Hebrew they are known as the Irin, "Watchers," also mentioned in the Old Testament Book of Daniel (chapter 4). The *Codex* mentions they are present in this last at the trial of Nebuchadnezzar, Daniel's king (195).

The Book of Jubilees describes them as large human beings that never sleep and remain forever silent. The fallen ones fell from grace and produced the Nephilim, but others are good. According to the Book of Enoch, the Gregori are angels dispatched to Earth simply to watch over the people.The book adds that the Grigori numbered a total of 200 with leaders bearing Biblical names:

> *These are the names of their chiefs: Samyaza, who was their leader, Urakabarameel, Akibeel, Tamiel, Ramuel, Danel, Azkeel, Saraknyal, Asael, Armers, Batraal, Anane, Zavebe, Samsaveel, Ertael, Turel, Yomyael, Azazyel (also known as Azazel). These*

were the prefects of the two hundred angels, and
the remainder were all with them.
(1 Enoch 7:9)

Perhaps this is why one of their leaders in the series is named Enoch, with others taking Bible names like Zachariah.

Jem adds that the Silent Brothers may be the original Black Friars of Blackfriars Bridge (*Clockwork Angel* 314). The Black Friars were a common name for the Dominican Order of friars – many places are named Blackfriars in honor of the order that would congregate there. They were preachers and teachers, focusing on spirituality as well as earthly poverty and humility, with black cloaks over their white robes. They seem parallels to the Silent Brothers thanks to their focus on separation, duty, and aid to the warriors.

Skeptron

In the demonic realm of *City of Heavenly Fire*, the teens discover another Idris, where the Shadowhunters lost the great battle and succumbed to demons. They also never made angel blades, but a single weapon with a single charge. This is the Skeptron, an iron rod tipped with a red jewel like Isabelle's. Skeptron is in fact the Greek word for scepter, or the royal baton. When Jace wields it, it sends out a pulse that destroys half the demons in the entire realm. "It was a brilliant, contained, icy flame, more light than heat, but a piercing light that shot through the whole room, limning everything in brilliance. Clary saw the demons turned to flaming silhouettes before they shuddered and exploded into ash" (*Heavenly Fire* 558).

Wrestles with God

In *Fallen Angel*, Camille paraphrases Ecclesiastes 6: 10 when she tells Simon that "Man cannot contend with the divine." Simon counters by recalling the story of Jacob in Genesis 32: 24– 30:

> *And Jacob was left alone; and there wrestled a man with him until the breaking of the day. And when he saw that he prevailed not against him, he touched the hollow of his thigh; and the hollow of Jacob's thigh was out of joint, as he wrestled with him. And he said, Let me go, for the day breaketh. And he said, I will not let thee go, except thou bless me. And he said unto him, What is thy name? And he said, Jacob. And he said, Thy name shall be called no more Jacob, but Israel: for as a prince hast thou power with God and with men, and hast prevailed. And Jacob asked him, and said, Tell me, I pray thee, thy name. And he said, Wherefore is it that thou dost ask after my name? And he blessed him there. And Jacob called the name of the place Peniel: for I have seen God face to face, and my life is preserved. And as he passed over Penuel the sun rose upon him, and he halted upon his thigh.* [as in, his thigh was injured] (24-31)

Simon does indeed wrestle with the divine when he hazards his life to summon the Angel Raziel – not just to save Jace, but because it's the right thing to do. He spends several books marked as outcast and outsider, rejected by the vampires as much as the Nephilim. "The biblical connections Clare makes to Simon are carefully chosen to reflect his Mark of Cain — his status as one on a journey, his connection to heaven (as its 'avenging arm' as Camille describes him), and one who will be blessed for his perseverance as he contends with forces 'mightier than he.'" (Spencer, Kindle Locations 1540-1545).

> *In the Book of Genesis, chapter 32, Peniel (or Penuel) is the name Jacob gives to a place where he wrestled an angel all night. He marks this sacred place, "for I have seen God face to face, and my life is preserved." It's a fitting title for chapter 19, in which Simon faces both Raphael and, in a sense, God by taking the Mark of Cain, and Jace wrestles Sebastian, who is, admittedly, the opposite of an angel.*
> (Spencer, Kindle Locations 1241-1244)

As a result, Jacob is crippled from the fight, just as Simon, after bargaining with Raziel, loses his heavenly protection. Jacob leaves the fight knowing he has God's blessing. Simon, with the sword of the angels, knows that he has a similar blessing, one he can use to preserve his friends and save the world.

17

The Film

For Cassandra Clare, who lists the Lord of the Rings trilogy as among her favorite films, it must have been a dream come true when Michael Lynne and Bob Shaye of Unique Features optioned her novel. These two producers were instrumental in setting up Peter Jackson's epic fantasy films at New Line Cinema. This time, they brought in Constantin Film to co-produce and help raise the necessary funding and partnerships to bring Clary's adventures to the big screen.
(Spencer, Kindle Locations 2023-2026)

In 2013, the film *The Mortal Instruments: City of Bones* arrived. It was quite faithful to the first book in its details (aside from a final battle in the Institute against the Forsaken). In real life, the stars Lily Collins and Jamie Campell Bower dated, leading to much fan excitement, though they broke up before the movie was released.

Nonetheless, somehow the content fell a bit flat and confused many new fans. Alec's struggle to come out, his hatred for Clary, his feelings for Magnus, were all rather curtailed. The jokes too, had mostly vanished. The creators were hoping for another *Twilight* or *Harry Potter* franchise, but the first film resulted in a poor box office and critical reception. With fans of the books also disappointed, the story was reimagined for television.

18

The Show

Shadowhunters, the fantasy television series based on *The Mortal Instruments,* was developed for television by Ed Decter. Hollie Overton, Michael Reisz, and Y. Shireen Razack are executive story editors. For this version, premiering on January 12, 2016 on Freeform (formerly ABC Family) the teens appear to be having much more fun. This time, the story is less squashed and there's more time for relationships and banter. The story was completely recast and rebooted from the beginning.

Constantin Film and TV head Martin Moszkowicz told *The Hollywood Reporter,* "It actually makes sense to do [the novels] as a TV series. There was so much from the book that we had to leave out of the *Mortal Instruments* film. In the series we'll be able to go deeper and explore this world in greater detail and depth" (Barraclough). The series is off to a strong start, and fans are more enthusiastic this time around.

Cast

- Katherine McNamara as Clary Fray
- Dominic Sherwood as Jace Wayland
- Alberto Rosende as Simon Lewis
- Matthew Daddario as Alec Lightwood

- Emeraude Toubia as Isabelle Lightwood
- Isaiah Mustafa as Luke Garroway
- Harry Shum Jr. as Magnus Bane

Recurring characters:

- Alan Van Sprang as Valentine Morgenstern
- Maxim Roy as Jocelyn Fray
- David Castro as Raphael Santiago
- Jon Cor as Hodge Starkweather
- Shailene Garnett as Maureen
- Lisa Marcos as Captain Susanna Vargas
- Vanessa Matsui as Dot
- Jade Hassouné as Meliorn
- Kaitlyn Leeb as Camille Belcourt

Episodes

1. The Mortal Cup – 12 January 2016

2. The Descent into Hell is Easy – 19 January 2016

3. Dead Man's Party – 26 January 2016

4. Raising Hell – 2 February 2016

5. "Moo Shu to Go" – 9 February 2016

6. "Of Men and Angels"- 16 February 2016

7. "Major Arcana"- 23 February 2016

8. "Bad Blood" – 1 March 2016

9. "Rise Up" – 8 March 2016

10. "This World Inverted" – 15 March 2016

11. "Blood Calls to Blood"- 22 March 2016

12. "Malec" – 29 March 2016

13. "Morning Star"- 5 April 2016

19

The Next Series

The three trilogies: two with Clary, Jace and their friends, one with their Victorian ancestors, continue to sell well, with several nonfiction guides by Clare and two books of short stories to round it out. *The Bane Chronicles* and *Shadowhunter Academy* were released story by story on the web in 2013 and 2015, taking advantage of new mediums while rounding out the Shadowhunters' world through its side characters.

Lady Midnight arrives in March 2016. It follows all the young Blackthorn children, their parents dead, their older sister exiled, and their older brother kidnapped by fairies. From age ten, Julian, the oldest, has been looking after the four younger children and his rather helpless uncle as well. His partner in this is the young warrior Emma Carstairs, the other central hero – she's on a mission to investigate her parents' deaths. Together they must solve the more immediate puzzle of why parabatai are forbidden to fall in love.

The Cold Peace and its harsh treatment of the fairies is also central. In *Shadowhunters Academy,* Mark Blackthorn says:

> *"I tried to be a Shadowhunter, even in the depths*
> *of Faerie, and what good did it do me? 'Show*
> *them what a Shadowhunter is made of!' What is*
> *a Shadowhunter made of, if they desert their own,*

if they throw away a child's heart like rubbish left on the side of the road? Tell me, Simon Lewis, if that is what Shadowhunters are, why would I wish to be one?"

"Because that's not all they are," Simon said.

"And what are faeries made of? I hear Shadowhunters say they are all evil now, barely more than demons set upon the earth to do wicked mischief." Mark grinned, something wild and fey in the grin, like sunlight glittering through a spiderweb. "And we do love mischief, Simon Lewis, and sometimes wickedness. But it is not all bad, to ride the winds, run upon the waves, and dance upon the mountains, and it is all I have left. At least the Wild Hunt wants me. Maybe I should show Shadowhunters what a faerie is made of instead."
("Bitter of Tongue")

Like the previous one, this series will alternate between two settings: This time with the lives of the children of the *Infernal Devices* heroes.

"James Herondale was the son of angels and demons," Catarina says in "Nothing but Shadows." "He was always fated to walk a difficult and painful path, to drink bitter water with sweet, to tread where there were thorns as well as flowers. Nobody could save him from that. People did try." The story follows him and Matthew Fairchild his parabatai, as well as their siblings, loves, and friends, as the next generation of teen heroes after the stars of *The Infernal Devices*. Though a large section of their family tree was published in *Clockwork Princess,* the author insists many details of history were lost and the family tree doesn't tell the whole story. James's story, as shown through a snippet of his life in the *Bane Chronicles,* appears to be largely inspired by *Great Expectations*, as his father's was by *A Tale of Two Cities*.

Beyond this, of course, there will be short stories, episodes, and endless celebrations of fan art, fan clubs and an entire web of creative works. The Shadowhunters are here…and they're only getting bigger.

Thought Catalog, it's a website.
www.thoughtcatalog.com

Social
facebook.com/thoughtcatalog
twitter.com/thoughtcatalog
tumblr.com/thoughtcatalog
instagram.com/thoughtcatalog

Corporate
www.thought.is

Works Cited

Aquinas, Thomas. *The Summa Theologica of St. Thomas Aquinas Second and Revised Edition*. Trans. Fathers of the English Dominican Province. 1920. http://www.newadvent.org/summa

Bane, Theresa. *Encyclopedia of Demons in World Religions and Cultures*. Jefferson, NC: McFarland, 2012.

Barraclough, Leo. "Constantin to Produce TV Series Based on *Mortal Instruments, Resident Evil* Franchises." *Variety,* 12 Oct 2014.

The Book of Enoch. Trans. R.H. Charles. London: Society for Promoting Christian Knowledge, 1917. The Sacred Texts Archive. http://www.sacred-texts.com/bib/boe/index.htm.

Child, Francis James. "Thomas the Rhymer." *The English and Scottish Popular Ballads*. Boston, New York, Houghton, Mifflin and Company, 1886-98. *The Sacred Texts Archive*. http://www.sacred-texts.com/neu/eng/child/ch037.htm.

Cirlot, J.E. *A Dictionary of Symbols*. New York: Routledge, 1971.

Clare, Cassandra. "Author Interview: Cassandra Clare," *The Mortal's Library,* 29 Aug 2010. http://themortalslibrary.blogspot.com/2010/08/author-interview-cassandra-clare.html?spref=tw.

–. "The Blackthorns and Co." March 6 2013. Blog Post. http://cassandraclare.tumblr.com/post/44598318611/the-blackthorns-and-co.

– . *Cassandra Clare's Clockwork Princess Bus Tour*. Menlo Atherton High School Performing Arts Center, Menlo Park, CA. 23 Mar 2013. Personal Appearance.

–. *City of Ashes*. New York: Simon & Schuster, 2008.

–. *City of Bones*. New York: Simon & Schuster, 2007.

–. *City of Fallen Angels*. New York: Simon & Schuster, 2011.

–. *City of Glass*. New York: Simon & Schuster, 2009.

–. *City of Heavenly Fire*. New York: Simon & Schuster, 2014.

–. *City of Lost Souls*. New York: Simon & Schuster, 2012.

–. "City of Fallen Angels chapter titles – Cassandra Clare's Blog" 18 Feb 2010 http://cassandraclare.livejournal.com/34970.html.

–. "City of Glass Chapter Titles." 9 Sept 2008. Blog Post. http://cassandraclare.livejournal.com/24361.html.

–. "Clockwork Prince Cover and Chapter Titles." 29 May 2011. Blog Post. http://cassandraclare.livejournal.com/54654.html.

–. *Clockwork Angel*. USA: Margaret K. McElderry Books, 2010.

–. *Clockwork Prince*. USA: Margaret K. McElderry Books, 2011.

–. *Clockwork Princess*. USA: Margaret K. McElderry Books, 2013.

–. "City of Glass: A Dark Transformation." *Extras, Outtakes/Deleted Scenes & Short Stories from The Mortal Instruments books! Goodreads*. 3 July 2012. http://www.goodreads.com/topic/show/945398-extras-outtakes-deleted-scenes-short-stories-from-the-mortal-instrume.

–. "FAQ." *Cassandra Clare: New York Times Bestselling Author*. http://www.cassandraclare.com/frequently-asked-questions/about-the-books.

–. "Fairies." Tumblr page Aug 2015 http://cassandraclare.tumblr.com/post/125527509109/faeries

–. "The Infernal Devices: Frequently Asked Questions" Shadowhunters.com. http://www.shadowhunters.com/theinfernaldevices/faq.php.

–. "Interview: Cassandra Clare." *The Reader's Quill*. 6 Nov 2008. http://www.readersquill.com/2008/11/interview-cassandra-clare.html.

–. "Introduction." Clare, *Shadowhunters and Downworlders* ix-xiii.

–. "Lady Midnight Excerpt." http://shadowhunters.com/excerpt-lady-midnight/

–. "Random Question." April 2012. Blog Post. http://cassandraclare.tumblr.com/post/27358116912/random-question-was-the-real-sebastian-verlac-a.

–. *The Shadowhunter's Codex*. USA: Margaret K. McElderry Books, 2013.

–. "Simon Lewis, Jewish Vampire." June 2012. Blog Post. http://cassandraclare.tumblr.com/post/31293907714/simon-lewis-jewish-vampire.

Clare, Cassandra and Maureen Johnson. "The Fiery Trial." *Tales from the Shadowhunter Academy*. Cassandra Clare, Sarah Rees Brennan, Maureen Johnson and Robin Wasserman. USA: Margaret K. McElderry Books, 2013. Kindle Edition.

Clare, Cassandra and Maureen Johnson. "The Rise of the Hotel DuMort." *The Bane Chronicles*. Cassandra Clare, Sarah Rees Brennan and Maureen Johnson. USA: Margaret K. McElderry Books, 2013. 201- 247.

Clare, Cassandra and Robin Wasserman. "Pale Kings and Princes." *Tales from the Shadowhunter Academy*. Cassandra Clare, Sarah Rees Brennan, Maureen Johnson and Robin Wasserman. USA: Margaret K. McElderry Books, 2013. Kindle Edition.

Clare, Cassandra and Robin Wasserman. "The Lost Herondale." *Tales from the Shadowhunter Academy*. Cassandra Clare, Sarah Rees Brennan, Maureen Johnson and Robin Wasserman. USA: Margaret K. McElderry Books, 2013. Kindle Edition.

Clare, Cassandra and Sarah Rees Brennan. "Bitter of Tongue." *Tales from the Shadowhunter Academy*. Cassandra Clare, Sarah Rees Brennan, Maureen Johnson and Robin Wasserman. USA: Margaret K. McElderry Books, 2013. Kindle Edition.

Clare, Cassandra and Sarah Rees Brennan. "Born to Endless Night." *Tales from the Shadowhunter Academy*. Cassandra Clare, Sarah Rees Brennan, Maureen Johnson and Robin Wasserman. USA: Margaret K. McElderry Books, 2013. Kindle Edition.

Clare, Cassandra and Sarah Rees Brennan. "Nothing but Shadows." *Tales from the Shadowhunter Academy*. Cassandra Clare, Sarah Rees Brennan, Maureen Johnson and Robin Wasserman. USA: Margaret K. McElderry Books, 2013. Kindle Edition.

Clare, Cassandra and Sarah Rees Brennan. "Vampires, Scones and Edmund Herondale." *The Bane Chronicles*. USA: Margaret K. McElderry Books, 2013. 99-147.

Clare, Cassandra and Sarah Rees Brennan. "What to Buy the Shadowhunter Who Has Everything" *The Bane Chronicles*. USA: Margaret K. McElderry Books, 2013. 347-389.

"Clockwork Angel: An exclusive Q&A with Cassandra Clare." *Novel Novice*. 18 Aug 2010. http://novelnovice.com/2010/08/18/clockwork-angel-an-exclusive-qa-with-cassandra-clare

Dionysius the Areopagite. *The Celestial Hierarchy. The Esoteric Archives.* http://www.esoteric.msu.edu/VolumeII/CelestialHierarchy.html.

Dante Alighieri. *The Divine Comedy*. Trans. Mark Musa. Indiana: Indiana University Press, 1995.

Davidson, G. *A Dictionary of Angels. Including the Fallen Angels.* USA: Free Press, 1994.

de Manhar, Nurho. *The Sefer Ha-Zohar or The Book of Light*. Ed. H.W. Percival. New York: Theosophical Publishing Company, 1914. *The Sacred Texts Archive.* http://www.sacred-texts.com/jud/zdm/zdm000.htm.

Epic of Gilgamesh. Trans. Maureen Gallery Kovacs. Electronic Edition by Wolf Carnahan, 1998. http://www.ancienttexts.org/library/mesopotamian/gilgamesh/tab6.htm.

Evans-Wentz, W.Y. *The Fairy- Faith in Celtic Countries*. London and New York: H. Froude, 1911. *The Sacred Texts Archive.* http://www.sacred-texts.com/ neu/ celt/ffcc/ffcc122.htm.

Frankel, Valerie Estelle. *Myths and Motifs of the Mortal Instruments*. USA: Zossima Press, 2013.

Hanauer, J.E. *Folk-lore of the Holy Land: Muslim, Christian and Jewish*. London: Duckworth and Co, 1907. *The Sacred Texts Archive.* http://www.sacred-texts.com/asia/flhl/index.htm.

Isidore of Seville. *The Etymologies of Isidore of Seville*. Ed. and trans. Oliver Berghof. Cambridge: Cambridge University Press, 2009.

http://ebooks.cambridge.org/
ebook.jsf?bid=CBO9780511482113.

Kipling, Rudyard. "The Hour of the Angel." *The Collected Poems of Rudyard Kipling*. USA: Wordsworth Editions, 1994. 767.

Konstantinos. *Werewolves: The Occult Truth*. USA: Llewellyn Worldwide, Ltd, 2010.

Link, Kelly and Holly Black. "Immortality and its Discontents." *Shadowhunters and Downworlders*. Dallas, TX: BenBella, Inc., 2012.

Lokrien. "What Are Runes." *Internet Book of Shadows*, 1999. *The Sacred Texts Archive*. http://www.sacred-texts.com/bos/bos064.htm

Lumpkin, Joseph B., ed. *The Lost Book of Enoch: A Comprehensive Transliteration of the Forgotten Book of the Bible*. Fifth Estate Publishers, 2004.

Mack, Carol K and Dinah. *A Field Guide to Demons, Fairies, Fallen Angels, and Other Subversive Spirits*. New York: Henry Holt and Company, 1998.

Mackenzie, Donald A. *Indian Myth and Legend*. London: Gresham Publishing Co., Ltd, 1913. http://www.sacred-texts.com/hin/iml/iml00.htm

Marlowe, Christopher. *Marlowe's Tragical History of Doctor Faustus*. Clarendon Press, 1887. The On-Line Books Page. http://onlinebooks.library.upenn.edu.

Milton, John. *Paradise Lost*. New York: The Modern Library, 2007.

"Of the Art Goetia." *The Lesser Key of Solomon*. Ed. Joseph H. Peterson. USA: Weiser Books, 2001. http://www.esotericarchives.com/solomon/goetia.htm.

Palgrave, Francis T., Ed. *The Golden Treasury*. 1875. http://www.bartleby.com/106/67.html.

Pausanias. *Description of Greece*. Trans. W H S. Jones. Loeb Classical Library. Cambridge, Massachusetts: Harvard University Press.

Philostratus. *The Life of Apollonius of Tyana.* Trans. F C. Conybeare. Loeb Classical Library 2 Vols. Cambridge, Massachusetts: Harvard University Press.

Pliny the Elder. *Natural History.* Trans. H. Rackham. Loeb Classical Library, 3 Volumes. Cambridge, Massachusetts: Harvard University Press.

Sepher Rezial Hemelach: *The Book of the Angel Raziel.* Ed. Steve Savedow. USA: Weiser Books, 2000.

Spencer, Liv. *Navigating the Shadow World: The Unofficial Guide to Cassandra Clare's The Mortal Instruments.* Toronto: ECW Press, 2013.

Trachtenberg, Joshua. *Jewish Magic and Superstition: A Study in Folk Religion.* New York: Behrman's Jewish Book House, 1939. *The Sacred Texts Archive.* http://www.sacred-texts.com/jud/jms/jms00.htm

Vinycomb, John. *Symbolic Creatures in Art with Special Reference to the Use in British Heraldry.* London: Chapman and Hall, Ltd. 1909. *The Sacred Texts Archive.* http://www.sacred-texts.com.

Walker, Barbara G. *The Woman's Dictionary of Symbols and Sacred Objects.* San Francisco: Harper, 1988.

Watkins, Alfred. *The Old Straight Track: Its Mounds, Beacons, Moats, Sites and Mark Stones.* London: Abacus, 1925.

Webster, Richard. *Encyclopedia of Angels.* USA: Llewellyn Publications, 2009.

Weyer, Johann. *Pseudomonarchia Daemonum, or Hierarchy of Demons. De Praestigiis Daemonum.* 1577. *Esoteric Archives.* http://www.esotericarchives.com/solomon/weyer.htm

Wilde. Lady Francesca Speranza. *Ancient Legends, Mystic Charms, and Superstitions of Ireland.* London: Ward & Downey, 1887. http://www.sacred-texts.com/neu/celt/ali/ali000.htm

About the Author

Valerie Estelle Frankel, MFA, is the author of many books on pop culture, including *Doctor Who and the Hero's Journey*, *Myths and Motifs of the Mortal Instruments*, and *How Game of Thrones Will End*. Many of her books focus on women's roles in fiction, from her heroine's journey guides *From Girl to Goddess* and *Buffy and the Heroine's Journey* to books like *Women in Game of Thrones* and *The Many Faces of Katniss Everdeen*. Once a lecturer at San Jose State University, she's now teaching English at Mission College. Come explore her research at www.vefrankel.com.